This book is dedicated to the wonderful support and joy brought to me by my wife Namaste and my five wonderful children Nadia, Saskia, Max, Anastasia, and Ivana.

Something In The Air

The story of Olga's mission

Tim Nicolai

Taggler Publications

First paperback edition printed 2014 in the United Kingdom

A catalogue record for this book is available from the British Library.

ISBN 978-0-9929996-0-5

Published by Taggler Publications

For more copies of this book, please email: Publications@tagglerindustries.com

Designed and Set by Integrated Graphics Ltd

Printed in Great Britain

CHAPTER ONE

It was a windy day. No, it was a very windy day, one of those days when you walk bent over forwards, as if you had a rope tied around your waist, and were towing a very large bus up a very steep hill.

Olga was generally very happy, as she usually was, but in an ideal world she could have done without quite so much wind. She got to the end of the park and sat down on the ground against one of twenty or so metal posts, which, she supposed, were there to stop cars sneaking in to the car park, by a way other than the prescribed.

As she sat, bolt upright, and with her back to the relentless wind, a strong metallic voice from just behind her ear said, 'Hello, my dear. How are you today?'

'Oh, I'm fine,' said Olga. 'How are you?'

'Actually I'm very pissed on today,' said the voice.

'Don't you mean pissed *off*? That's what most people say.'

'My dear girl, I assure you that what I mean is pissed *on*.'

'Is that the same thing?'

'Well, I've never really understood what pissed off means, but please understand that being the first post at the end of a large building, adjacent to a large park, frequented by a multitude of dogs, in all shapes and sizes. I am probably the world's greatest authority on the meaning of pissed on.'

'How do you think I feel?' said a deep gravelly voice from somewhere just underneath Olga's bottom.

'Oh, don't you start – it's your job to get walked on!' said the post. 'This is a private conversation, so please butt out!'

'I know what pissed off means, and I'm only ten,' said Olga, proudly and perhaps just a little bit precociously.

Olga was indeed ten-going-on-thirty. She was plain, yet there was a strange, almost magical, knowing look in her eyes that could speak to anyone – and stranger than that, to anything. Olga had communication, like a river has water, and chewy things have chewiness.

Everyone and everything in the whole world, with absolutely no exceptions at all, could speak to Olga if they so desired. Stranger still, Olga had a unique disposition – this was by far the most special thing about Olga. Olga didn't mind chatting to anyone or anything, and perhaps I ought to mention at this point that Olga didn't think it was at all strange.

I do, just in case you think I am completely bonkers. Anyway, I was about to tell you about Olga's disposition. I said she was plain – but beneath that, there is something in her eyes, a kind of alertness that could easily be mistaken for arrogance, were it not for a vast enveloping warmth. I really don't think that anyone, or indeed as we can see, anything, could look into Olga's eyes, and not want to talk with her. Olga also has a gigantic capacity for acceptance and understanding, an ability to take on board the wildest of ideas and find them completely plausible, whilst at the same time remaining shrewd and never even slightly gullible.

If I were to say to you, 'Hi! My name is Yiptop and I am from the planet Zog. I'm not really supposed to travel this far, and if my parents knew, they would go ballistic...' you would probably say something like, 'Yeah, right! You're nuts, mister!' But Olga would say something like, 'Cool, nice to meet you, Yiptop, what are you up to? How did you get here? Are you staying long? Do you want to come to tea?' In fact, something very much like that is exactly what she said when she first met Yiptop.

You see, Olga has this amazing ability to accept the very strangest of things. Perhaps not very much more amazing is that the very strangest of things seem perfectly aware of this and make a bee line for her, in much the way they make a bee line *away* from us.

'Well, you're very clever, then,' said the post.

'How old are you?' said Olga.

'Oh, I'm as old as the hills.'

'When I was little, my dad took me to see Father Christmas. We went into his grotto, and he sat me on his knee, and said, "how old are you, little girl?" I said, "I'm not old, I'm new". I told my dad this, and he said, "Olga, you're a very strange little girl, aren't you?"

'Do you think I'm very strange?' Olga asked the post.

'With the very greatest respect, my dear,' said the post, 'you are sat down, on this very windy Thursday afternoon, chatting to a cast-iron post. I think that qualifies you for most definitions of strange.'

'You spoke to me first,' said Olga.

'Oh, I speak to everyone,' said the post.

'Then how does that make me strange?' Olga asked.

'That qualifies you for three counts of strangeness. One, you heard me. Two, you listened to me. And three, you answered me.'

'That's only two counts.'

'How?'

'Hearing and listening are the same thing.'

'I'm very glad you said that.'

'Why?'

'Because I was beginning to wonder if you really were ten years old. They are not the same at all. Hearing happens by accident. It requires no effort at all on your part. Listening, however, is quite different. I, and a lot of other things for that matter, happen to think that it's really quite important to know the difference. Please don't be offended – you are listening, and that's the main thing.'

'You're sort of sage-like, aren't you?' said Olga. 'I don't really know what sage-like means, but I have heard adults say it about clever people. I've seen my mum mixing sage with onions and putting it in a chicken's bottom before cooking it, so I can't quite understand how it goes with cleverness. Why did you speak to me?'

'Wrong question.'

'What do you mean?'

'Well, I've already told you that I speak to everyone, so I haven't done anything unusual. The question you really need to ask is why are you speaking to me.'

'Shouldn't I ask myself that one?'

'Well, you can if you like.'

'I just did.'

'And what was your answer?'

'I don't know. That is, my answer is – I don't know.'

'Oh, that doesn't surprise me.'

'So I am asking *you*. Why am I hearing you?'

'Good question, Olga. Very good question indeed. Absolutely brilliant question, possibly the best question I have heard in a very, very long time.'

'You don't know the answer, do you?'

'Well I....'

'Ha ha!' laughed Olga. 'I know you either don't know the answer, or you don't know how to tell me the answer, because you're stalling. My dad does that when he doesn't know the answer.'

'Oh, alright! I don't know the answer, but I know it's not to do with anything I've done.'

'How do you know that?'

'Because I can easily eliminate me.'

'Don't do that! I'm just getting to know you.'

'I mean eliminate me, in that I won't be exclusive to the situation.'

'You do make things complicated.'

'Well, I don't mean to, they just seem to go that way sometimes. What I mean is…'

'I know what you mean; we were interrupted by the pathway, and you were very rude to him, or it.'

'Yes, that's right. I don't like being interrupted, especially when something very strange and interesting is happening. But before we go completely off the subject, that puts the strangeness squarely in your court.'

'It could be in my jeans, this listening or hearing. My dad says that if your mum, dad or granddad or someone has a particular kind of cleverness, it can get into your jeans and you will be good at it too. You don't have to be wearing your jeans – it gets in anyway. Even if you buy new jeans because you've outgrown the old ones, you will still be good at these things.'

'Yes, dear – that's all very interesting. I'm not sure you've got it quite right, but what does that have to do with listening?'

'I was just telling you. You see, my dad is very clever with his ears – he works with his ears. He listens to the engines on people's cars and says things like "your camshaft has gone," or "you have a big end," or "your tappers need something". He's called a motor engine ear. So that's probably it – my granddad was a motor engine ear too. It's got into my jeans now, and I'm stuck with it. I suppose if you never ever wore jeans you might get away with it, but then it would probably just get into your jumper or something. I suppose everyone wears jeans though, don't they?'

'Well, I would probably look rather silly in jeans,' said the post.

Olga looked at her watch and saw that it was already a quarter past four.

'Blast!' said Olga. 'I should be home by now. My mum will go mad!' She stood up to go.

'You will come back, won't you?' said the post.

'Yes, tomorrow after school,' said Olga.

'Well, 'bye for now,' said the post.

''Bye,' said Olga, as she bent forward to plough her way home.

As Olga ploughed her way through the dreadful wind, she wasn't thinking as we would. We would think, 'That was scary and weird! I need to get home to my mum and lie down for a while with my favourite blanket! I just had a conversation with a cast-iron post, momentarily interrupted by a gravel pathway. What is happening to me?'

No, as I already said, Olga isn't like us. And considering all the very strange things that were about to enter her hitherto relatively uncomplicated life, it is really just as well that she isn't like us.

In her very-unlike-us way, Olga was meandering happily home, thinking, 'What a very nice charming and friendly iron post!' How silly she felt for not asking its name. She wondered if it ever felt cold and lonely, stuck out by the park all the time. She was also getting rather excited at the prospect that there could now be lots of other interesting, fun, and intelligent things she could chat with. Not that she was about to test it out immediately, and try and talk to every lamppost or garden wall that she passed. Olga was, unlike us, just about the most patient person you could imagine. She would probably not speak to anything until it spoke to her. Frankly, if I myself had had such an amazing and life changing revelation, I would be talking to everything and everyone with the excited stammering rapidity of a twelve-year-old who had gone to school one morning, only to find it closed down.

The home that Olga was meandering towards was about as ordinary as you could imagine. She had two quite ordinary parents – one of each, unlike some of her friends. It was in an ordinary street in an ordinary town and, as far as most people were concerned, in an ordinary world.

If Olga's parents knew anything about most of what Olga thought about or encountered in her life, they would be beside themselves – not an expression I have ever heard or used without a slight chuckle at how we come up with such sayings. Imagine for one second hearing some quite disturbing news, then looking to the right or left and finding that you are in fact beside yourself. If the world was really as simple and ordinary as most people seem happy to assume, I don't think we would have such strange sayings. Fortunately for Olga's parents, they had absolutely no idea what Olga thought about; she had recently taken to sparing them anything that she determined they wouldn't cope with. She was very perceptive about what people could cope with.

'Hi, Mum! Sorry I'm a bit late – it was really windy,' said Olga.

'Hello, sweetheart,' said Olga's mum. 'What have you been up to? It's after half past four.'

'Nothing,' said Olga, slightly peeved that her mother hadn't listened, as usual, and seemed continually intent on stating the obvious, like what time it was.

It wasn't that Olga didn't like her mum. She loved her mum and dad dearly. It was just that she didn't really have anything in common with them, and she felt that they couldn't get a grip on what she was about. That was, in fairness to them, partly because her early efforts to share her thoughts with them had resulted in their complete confusion, and partly because of her uncomfortable sessions with a child psychologist, which quite frankly she had no desire to repeat.

'Your dad will be home in a few minutes, darling,' said Olga's mum.

'That's nice,' said Olga. 'He's early today.'

'Yes, sweetheart. He's taking me out to dinner. It's our wedding anniversary today.'

'That's nice, Mum. Will you be dressing up? Can I help you choose something, and make you look really beautiful?'

'Yes, darling – that would be fun.'

Olga couldn't really be less interested in how anyone looked, but she always offered to do things like that. Firstly because it made her mum happy, but also because it made her mum and her dad feel that she was almost the normal little girl they had hoped for. It also kept a good distance between her and that dreadful shrink. Just then an awful thought occurred to Olga.

'Who's babysitting, mum?' said Olga.

'Jenny, darling,' said Olga's mum.

'Oh no, not her again! All she ever does is put the telly on some stupid celeb show about celebs scratching their bums and what we should all read into it, and spends the whole evening eating crisps and chocolate. It's surprising she's not called Jenny the elephant!'

'Now, darling. It's not nice to say things like that about people.'

'Well, I don't know how they're ever going to change if we don't. Anyway, I'll probably go to bed and leave her to it.'

Unlike lots of ten-year-olds (and unlike lots of ten-year-olds was how Olga was happy to be) no-one ever needed to send Olga to bed. Ever since she could walk and talk she had been quite happy to spend time in her room with her own thoughts, and drift off to sleep when she was tired.

'Hi, everyone!' shouted Olga's dad as he came in through the front door.

'Hi, Dad!' shouted Olga back.

'Hi, darling!' said Olga's mum. 'Olga is going to help me get ready. I've finished with the bathroom, and Jenny will be round at seven o'clock.'

Olga spent the next couple of hours eating her tea and helping her mum look beautiful. At seven o'clock Jenny arrived and Olga's mum and dad went off for their evening out. Olga managed to sidestep Jenny's offer to share the pleasure of 'Celebrities Stranded on a Traffic Island', a televisual experience Olga felt she could comfortably live without. She went up to her room, and settled down to think peacefully, thinking being just about Olga's favourite pastime, although she actually disliked the word pastime, as she felt that time did that perfectly well without any assistance from her. By about eight thirty, Olga had drifted off to sleep, only to be awakened by a *tap-tap* at her bedroom window and a little voice calling her name.

CHAPTER TWO

Thinking is another thing that separated Olga from most other people. She would later discover that it didn't quite separate her from trees as much as she would have liked. Olga really rather liked trees, but would never have felt quite comfortable being too much like one. There isn't much that would cause Olga to freak out, but that would get fairly close to it. Trees were excellent thinkers, and since time immemorial, had never lost the art; in fact, they had refined it considerably. People, however, throughout time (well, that's not entirely true – throughout so-called civilised time would be more accurate), had slowly, yet very determinedly reduced the process of thinking, so much as to render it almost useless. Trees are quite different. They have even evolved to resemble physically a typical thought. I can understand if you are struggling with quite what I'm on babbling about here, but bear with me.

Trees have refined the process of thought so much that some of them spend the whole of their considerably long lives just thinking about thinking. Then the whole of this process is passed on, in its entirety, to each offspring tree, to be continued for further lifetimes. Furthermore, all thinking is shared with all other trees.

So you see, every tree shares every thought with every other tree, which also shares every thought that has ever been thought by any previously existing tree, and then thinks its own thoughts, and so the process goes on.

In fact, this means that if you were ever unfortunate enough to have a conversation with a tree, you could actually stop in the middle of it, walk away, and carry on exactly where you left off with a completely different tree, even if it was in another part of the world. I can quite understand if you find this idea a little bit scary; the whole concept would be very scary indeed, were it not for this fact. Trees are exceptionally good at thinking, mostly because that's all they do. A tree couldn't possibly be less interested in doing anything about any thought that occurred to it. A tree may very occasionally be persuaded to share the odd thought with another thing or person – usually an extremely simple thought; only a tree would be capable of understanding a complex thought. They think for thought's sake, and that's it. Apart from the mundane but fairly important task of providing the Air with some stability and oxygen, for which the Air never seems quite grateful enough, Thought is what they are for.

You could easily run away with the idea that trees are really all one thing – it's true that they share consciousness, but they manage, in a way which would really be beyond our understanding, to retain individuality. I suppose you could look at them as a very large number of computers, all networked together in a hub, the hub being the planet we live on.

Mentioning computers to a tree, by the way, would not be a very good idea at all. Trees believe, from their great thought, in *the proper order of things*. As I have already said, they really couldn't be bothered to do anything about it, but they nonetheless believe it. In this *proper order of things,* they believe that they are the computers of the world. They are not very happy that mankind has completely ignored them since the beginning of civilisation and invented their own rather pathetic and simple computers. Furthermore, someone has plagiarised their wonderfully clever idea of universal networking – which, for several million years, they have regarded as The Worldwide Web – and called it the Internet.

If ever trees could be bothered to do anything at all, the very first thing they would do is complain about this and show everyone how terribly cross they are about it.

To be properly fair to people, they have capacity for original thought and creativity – nothing else on the planet has that facility. Lately, however, they weren't doing any more with that capacity than the trees were, in practice, doing with theirs.

'Olga!' said the little voice at Olga's bedroom window. *Tap-tap*. 'Olga! Can you hear me? It's me – Yiptop!'

Yiptop was hanging from the window sill by his hands and had his smiley pixie face pressed against the glass. This was his normal mode of arrival. Olga was puzzled by this as her room was upstairs. She hadn't got round to asking about it yet – there were always more pressing things to ask.

In his world, intellectually, he would be about the equivalent of a fourteen year old in ours. If you didn't know he was an alien from Zog, you would, without very close observation, just see him as a cute pixie-like little boy, perhaps a little jaundiced, about the height of the average fifteen-year-old. His ears were just slightly too round, and he had long fingers a pianist would die for – although to my knowledge so far, he couldn't play the piano at all and had expressed no desire to learn. If, however, you knew he was an alien from Zog, it would be more obvious to you that he was not quite of this world. Yiptop's appearance lived in that sort of middle ground, where, depending on what you thought, it could be regarded as quite strange or quite normal, but not much in between.

'Yiptop! Where have you been? I haven't seen you for ages,' said Olga, gleeful at the sight of her favourite friend.

'Let me in and I'll tell you. It's quite tricky having a conversation while I'm hanging on to your windowsill.'

'Sorry. I'll open it now,' said Olga, getting up to open the window. 'Climb in, and don't make too much noise – Jenny is downstairs. She's probably engrossed in "The 101 Best 101 Best" by now. Where's your spaceship?'

'You always call it a spaceship! It's an LIC, a light interplanetary craft, and it's behind the shed in the garden. A spaceship wouldn't fit anywhere in this city. the last one I went in had six and a half square miles of multiplanetary wildlife parks.'

This was the third time Yiptop had visited Olga. The first time, he had explained where he had come from and told her a little bit about space. It was three weeks ago, on a sunny Sunday afternoon. Olga's parents had gone to a barbecue at a neighbour's house down the road. They had made some small efforts to persuade Olga to go with them, but quickly realised that as usual there was not much point. If there was one thing Olga really disliked, it was silly parties full of silly people, talking about the car they have just bought, the size of their television screen, football, golf, and handbags. Olga found all this stuff not only very boring, but actually quite distasteful.

Olga already knew that Emily wouldn't be there –
Emily was Olga's favourite person. She might have gone if
Emily had been going. Even at the age of ten, Olga had
decided that there were much more important things to
occupy her mind-space than listening to adults partying. A
couple of hours' peaceful contemplation on a nice sunny
afternoon were probably not the coolest idea from most ten-
year-olds' point of view, but then Olga wasn't really very
much like most ten-year-olds.

And so it was that Olga had been at home when
Yiptop had turned up in her garden, landing quite silently
behind the garden shed.

He had tapped on her shoulder and said, ' Hi. My
name is Yiptop I am from the planet Zog. I'm not
really supposed to travel this far. If my parents knew,
they would go ballistic.'

'Cool! Nice to meet you, Yiptop. What are you up to? How did you get here? Are you staying long? Do you want to come to tea?'

'You are crazy,' said Yiptop.

'Excuse me,' said Olga. 'You turn up in my garden from another planet. I politely ask you to tea, and you tell me I'm crazy!'

'Oh, I'm sorry! Please don't be upsot.'

'I think you mean *upset*.'

'Yes, that's rote – upsot.'

'That's right.'

'That's rote. Don't get upsot, I mean.'

'*Upset!*' said Olga a little louder.

'Do you have some waiters? I really need a dronk.'

'We don't have waiters. We get our own drinks.'

'No, can you get me a dronk of waiter plaese.'

'Don't you mean a drink of water?'

'That's rote. A dronk of waiter, please.'

Olga went off into the house to get Yiptop a glass of water, leaving him in the garden looking a little troubled.

'Here you are,' said Olga, coming back with a large glass of water which she handed to Yiptop.

'Think you. I'll be butter in a minute,' said Yiptop, and drank the whole glassful in one gulp.

Yiptop didn't function like us. He didn't ever need to eat food – his body and mind were very highly developed. He only needed water. The first symptom of water deficiency was a profound effect on his very sophisticated speech system. Water would correct this straight away.

'Are you okay now?' asked Olga, a little concerned.

'Yes, I'm fine now. I need water all the time. If I don't get it, my speech goes all wrong,' said Yiptop, very straight-faced and a little embarrassed.

'I noticed that,' said Olga, smirking a little too much.

'It was very funny. Anyway I asked you some questions and I'm dying to know the answers. This is so exciting! I knew there was life on other planets. All the adults say there isn't, but I knew there was. They have no imagination.'

'Okay – what am I up to? Just having fun, and being very naughty, I'm not supposed to be here, and if your parents knew, they would go ballistic…'

'If my parents heard me talking to an alien, they would go ballistic. Where are you from?'

'I told you that. I'm from Zog.'

'You may as well say you're from Boggey Boo. Where is Zog?'

'If I was from Boggey Boo you would be much better off not talking to me, or even for that matter not looking at me. How do you know about Boggey Boo? It's a quite insignificant planet in the middle of nowhere.'

'I don't know about Boggey Boo I just made it up, I may as well have said Diddley Squat.'

'Diddley Squaten.'

'No, Diddley Squat.'

'There is no Diddley Squat – it's called Diddley Squaten.'

'This is getting really silly. I mention two nonsense words and you tell me they're planets.'

'Its not surprising, is it? There are four hundred and sixty three billion planets in the known universe, not to mention I don't know how many in the unknown universe. Almost anything you say is likely to be a planet somewhere.'

'Where's the unknown universe?'

'I don't know. No-one does. That's why it's called the unknown universe – no-one has found it yet.'

'So, we have Zog, Boggey Boo, and Diddley Squaten.'

'Do you want me to go through them all? It will take a while. Actually, if you started now, making up random words, you would be long dead before you ran out of planets, and you wouldn't get many wrong.'

'Do you know them all?'

'Of course I know them all – I'm from Zog!'

'What's being from Zog got to do with it?'

'Zoggers have infinite memory.'

'Infantile, more like! What's the point in memorising four hundred and sixty three billion planet names?'

'There's no *point*. We just can't help it we remember everything – we have infinite memory.'

'Right, so you're from Zog. Where is Zog?'

'Section 436725, next to Zoggy.'

'It must be a long way away.'

'No, it's just around the corner.'

'Even I know that there is no planet Zog just around the corner, and I'm only ten.'

'Well, it is in fact the nearest planet to Earth.'

'No, it isn't. Mars is.'

'Mars is miles away.'

'No, it's not. It's in our solar system. Even I know that, and...'

'You're only ten! Look at this.'

Yiptop produced a flat screen from nowhere. Olga decided not to ask how at this point.

'On this screen is a plan of your town. You live here,' said Yiptop, pointing to the screen.

'Yes, I know where I live.'

'And you're only ten!' said Yiptop, smirking, a bit like Olga had done earlier. 'This is where you live, and this,' he said, pointing to another part of the screen, 'Is the next street.'

'Yes.'

'So now, stand up and turn around full circle.'

Olga did so.

'Right,' said Yiptop, 'did you see the next street?'

'No, of course not. There are trees and houses and stuff in the way.'

Yiptop pointed to the screen again.

'Did you see that building there – the tall one?'

'Yes, of course. You can see that from anywhere.'

'Well, this is a bit like space. Your scientists think it's really simple, but actually it isn't at all the way it looks. It's got all kinds of twists and turns, and things in the way, which are too dark to see, because they don't reflect light or other radiation. So, it looks like Mars is near, like that building – but Zog is nearer, like the next street.'

The flat screen disappeared, and again Olga decided not to mention it for now.

'Okay,' said Olga in her delightfully accepting and trusting way, 'I'll take your word for it. Zog is next door, Babble Do Do.'

'Just Babble Do actually, ancient planet sector 6574.'

'Just testing!' said Olga, giggling with excitement.

'What are you doing here, then?'

'Just riding around in my LIC and having fun. I'm not supposed to be visiting third universe planets though, but lots of us sneak in for a bit of fun – have done for generations.'

'So this is a third universe planet, then?'

'Yep.'

'What's a first universe planet, then?'

'Zog, for a start. We are much more advanced than you.'

'But you still talk rubbish, when you need a glass of water, though!' said Olga, recapturing the smirking ground. 'What's this sneaking-in-for-fun thing, then? Sounds very mischievous to me.'

'It's just a bit of taking the Mickey. Never any harm, and we never interfere. Well, not much.'

'That's not very nice, coming to a third universe planet just to make fun of us.'

'It is fun, really fun! Zoggers have been doing it ever since we had interplanetary travel.'

'What kind of things do you do?'

'All kinds of stuff.'

'Like?'

'First I materialise my view screen, so I can watch the fun. Then I might do some things that go bump in the night – that's an old one, but it works really well. Then there's making big circles in fields.'

'I've heard about things that go bump in the night. People think it's ghosts.'

'There's no ghosts. It's just aliens, having some fun,' Zog said. 'There have been some classics, famous all over the known universe. One of the very old people on Zog – this was really naughty – put a really big Zog fish in a lake in Scotland. It was only there for a couple of days, but your people have been looking for it ever since.'

'The Loch Ness monster!'

'Yes, that's what you call it.'

'Yiptop, that's really very naughty!'

'It's harmless. If we were as bad as some Earth people, we would do much worse things. Spiders in the bath are a great one, because to this day your scientists won't even talk about it. People just accept it, and it's completely impossible!'

'No, it isn't! I've found a spider in my bath.'

'Yes, I know – I put it there!' said Yiptop, giggling with pride.

'Then how is it impossible? Everyone knows they crawl up the waste pipe. There's even a nursery rhyme about it.'

The ubiquitous screen appeared again, and again Olga said nothing. On the screen was a diagram of a waste pipe, just under the bath.

'Look,' said Yiptop. 'That u-shaped pipe has water in it. The water fills the bottom of the pipe. If the spider crawled up the pipe, he would then have to dive into the water, swim underwater a little way, then resurface and climb out into the bath. Spiders don't swim under water, and as far as I know, they definitely don't dive.' Yiptop let go of the screen and it disappeared. Olga almost commented this time.

'This is all a bit worrying, really. I mean, finding out that there are other planets, very nearby, with much more advanced people than us. There must be bad people on these planets, that might want to attack us or take us over, make us into slaves to dig mines for them,' said Olga.

'You mean like some of your people do to less-developed people on your planet.'

'I suppose so. There are bad people everywhere.'

'No, there aren't!' said Yiptop incredulously.

'Of course there are. There are always bad people.'

'On planets that have reached a stage of development, where they have achieved interplanetary travel, they have learned the very simple fact that there is simply no point being bad, it just makes everybody unhappy and it's horrible. A bit of naughtiness is one thing. But not nastiness – that's awful.'

'So nothing to worry about, then? No Star Wars and stuff?'

'Nope, pure fiction. Can't happen. All you ever need to worry about is already right here on your own planet.'

'Like what my dad calls steroid gorillas. You see them hanging out at street corners, talking about how big their muscles are, and being aggressive and horrible to anyone who goes by. My dad says you really don't need to worry about people like that – gorillas are big and strong, but he hadn't noticed that they were running things.'

'I know what you mean. You are a very special ten-year-old Earth girl. There won't be people like that one day, but I can't help noticing that on your planet you have taken nastiness to new levels in other ways as well.'

'How do you mean?'

'You are still at the stage where you think that the earth needs running. It's quite laughable for me. You all live on this massive planet, which was here several billions of years before you evolved, and you seem to have somehow got the idea that it needs you to run it.'

'You mean we don't need to run it?'

'Who do think ran it before you lot evolved?'

'Someone else?'

'Silly! It has all the elements to run itself. All you have to do is leave it alone, and try not to get in its way. In fact it's one of the oldest sayings in the known universe – "the best way to run a planet is to let it run itself and try not to get in its way". The not-get-in-its-way part, however, is the bit that takes most understanding, even after you have learned the let-it-run-itself bit. It usually takes reasonably advanced beings a few million years to get that one.'

'Do you need a glass of water?' said Olga.

'Better had,' said Yiptop, 'just in case.'

Olga went to the bathroom and fetched a large glass of water, which Yiptop drank in one gulp.

CHAPTER THREE

'I'm glad you came today,' said Olga. 'I've had a very strange day, and I'm sure, with your infinite-memory brain, you may be able to make more sense of it than I have.'

'You'd better tell me all about it, then,' said Yiptop, looking very interested.

'I was walking home from school today. It was very windy, so when I got to the end of the park, I sat down against one of the metal posts, when suddenly, it spoke to me.'

'Very interesting! What did it say?'

'It just sort of chatted, and moaned a bit about dogs. Then it seemed a bit surprised that I could hear it.'

'I expect it would have been extremely surprised that you had heard it.'

'We sort of worked out that it was because my dad was an engine ear.'

Yiptop couldn't quite work out what that could possibly have to do with it, but like Olga with the screen, he decided not to go there for now. 'Hmm,' he said.

'Come on then, clever clogs. Apply your great brain to something other than taking the Mickey out of poor third universe creatures like me.'

'Okay! Keep your hair on. I'm thinking, and what I'm thinking is, I really shouldn't be talking about this. So how have you been? Anything else happening?'

'You can't do this to me! The strangest thing that's ever happened to me in my life – even, if that's possible, stranger than meeting you – and now the other strangest thing in my life won't talk about it!'

'I'm in a very difficult position here.'

'You put yourself in it. You're not supposed to be here in the first place, and now that you're here, you want to pick and choose what you tell me and what you don't.'

'For one thing, I'm not really sure you'll understand. Secondly, if you have somehow been allowed to hear residuals, something very strange and a little bit scary is going on.'

'If you find it strange and scary, how do you think this little third-universe girl feels?'

'Okay then. I'll try to explain as much as I can, but it's quite a long story, and first of all I will have to relieve you of the odd misconception.'

'Who's the odd Miss Conception?'

'See what I mean? Misconception means things that you think are real and aren't, and things that are not the way you think they are.'

'There! See? I understand all that and I'm only…'

'..ten – yes, okay. But you must never tell anyone any of this.'

'Okay. I promise.'

'You know about how my memory is.'

'Yes – infinite, and that means no limits, at all.'

'Right, well your memories aren't at all like that. In fact your people are at the stage of development where they believe that it is what they remember that matters. Couldn't be further from the truth. Because of this…'

'….misconception,' said Olga proudly.

'Yes, very good – it's what they forget that is most important, mostly because that is what's infinite. They also think that they are the most knowledgeable things on the planet. It may surprise you to know that they are not, by quite a long way.'

Olga found all this a little bit incredible, but decided to hear the whole story before she dismissed it as nonsense.

Yiptop continued. 'The two most knowledgeable things are the trees and the air. Next come the residuals, but it's fair to say that the residuals get all their information from people. They just have infinite memory, like the trees. Oh, and me, the Air, well that's quite different, we won't go into that now.

'No need to be big-headed.'

'People will eventually evolve to have infinite memory, it just won't be for a long time.'

Yiptop was secretly thinking that for certain people, the time might be coming sooner than expected, but he definitely wasn't going to say anything about that at all.

'You see,' said Yiptop, 'when a planet starts, the first thing it needs is air. Air is like a big thing that wraps itself around a planet, sort of hugs it, to keep everything from flying off. Forget gravity, that's not it at all – in fact it doesn't exist. The next things it needs are trees. Trees are like big computers all connected together and they run everything and make it work. All this is in place long before there are any people.'

'And next come residuals, whatever they are,' said Olga excitedly and a little precociously trying to anticipate Yiptop.

'No, please listen. Next come people,' said Yiptop, a little more firmly than he had meant to. 'You can't have residuals until you have people. Residual means left over – they are all the things people forget. Well, they are just things really, like old stones, posts, old buildings. What they are really supposed to do is carry all the things people forget, until the Air tells them to start passing it on. What actually happens in practise is that they chatter on and on all the time, until the Air decides it's time to start people listening, which is the worrying bit.'

'Why is that the worrying bit? I'm quite concerned because it seems to be the bit that's connected to me.'

'It's worrying because it's not time yet.'

'How do you know it's not time?'

'It's easy. Your people are very obviously not ready.'

'So why has it happened then, Yiptop?'

'I honestly don't know.'

'Well how am I supposed to find out, then?'

'I'm not sure,' said Yiptop, looking very much as if he wished he hadn't started. 'But there must be some kind of problem or something. I think you had better tell the post about me, and ask him to tell you more.'

'But you told me not to tell anyone about any of this.'

'Yes,' said Yiptop, lightening up a bit. 'I told you not to tell any*one*, not any*thing*.'

'This is so exciting! And a bit scary. I'll talk with the post on my way home from school tomorrow.'

'Good. I hope I haven't made you worry,' said Yiptop.

'It's okay. I don't worry about things. My dad says if you can do something about it, do it, and if you can't, don't worry.'

'Your dad sounds like a very wise man.'

'He's really cool. How are things on Zog?'

'Same as always. My mum is working on a book about the significance of moons in early planetary development, and my dad just plays golf.'

'People play golf on Zog?' exclaimed Olga in utter d isbelief.

'It's a very popular classic sport and Zoggers are very good at it.'

'Your mum sounds very intellectual, like a professor or something.'

'She is. She's professor of lunar studies at the Department of Sociology at the Planetary University of Zog.'

'Do you get on well with your parents, Yiptop?' asked Olga.

'I suppose so, but it's not like having friends. I don't think kids are meant to really get on with their parents. What do you think?'

'I agree, my parents think I'm a bit crazy.'

'You are crazy!' said Yiptop, laughing in his cutest pixie-like manner.

'I'm not crazy, it's just that crazy things happen around me. I can't help it. I don't walk around with a sign on my head, saying "all aliens and sundry objects that feel like chatting, queue up in front of me". It just happens.'

'No, but you do have a sign inside your head that says "anyone accepted, I don't prejudge anyone, anything, or any concept".'

'Is that crazy?'

'Some people would think so.'

'But what do you think?'

'I think it's cool, really cool!'

Being a boy, that was just about as nice as he felt comfortable being towards a girl, and he visibly tightened his shoulders, and slightly deepened his voice for the next sentence. Of course, none of this was lost on Olga. She didn't miss anything.

'I have to go,' said Yiptop, feeling slightly uncomfortable, 'but I will come back tomorrow and find out what the post has to say. This is quite the most intriguing thing that has ever happened.'

Yiptop climbed back through the window and waved to Olga, who waved back and smiled.

'Bye!' shouted Olga, in one of those shouting whispers that only ten-year-olds seem to manage.

Olga climbed back into bed and was asleep within a few minutes, with far more on her mind than was really fair for a ten-year-old girl. Even if she was quite the brightest and special ten-year-old.

CHAPTER FOUR

Most girls of Olga's age listened to Radio 1 these days. Unusually, Olga had remarkably refined taste in music, art, and food – in most things, in fact.

She really couldn't be bothered with sampled and remixed nonsense, overdubbed with some puerile and lyrically deficient rapper – or worse, gangster rapper, prattling on about ''ow much me luv me beech an 'ow cool me ees wiv all me bling'.

That's not to say Olga didn't like some of the same things as other ten-year-old girls; she did find some of the more tuneful songs by some of the more recent girly groups quite pleasant in a girly-sort-of-way.

But in the main, Olga's musical taste went back to the sixties and seventies. (In fact, although she hadn't yet made the connection, it was rooted in 1969, and not coincidentally, it was directly linked to man's visit to the moon – but more of that later.)

She had heard and liked some people called Crosby, Stills, Nash and Young, James Taylor, Carole King, and on the more upbeat side she rather liked the surreal quality of Pink Floyd. The only fairly modern music she found deeply enjoyable were Beck and Radiohead.

Artistically, she loved most Impressionist painters, particularly Monet. On the other hand she also loved Dali, Picasso, and David Hockney. She adored Jackson Pollock and really felt she had a good idea of what he was getting at. In fact, add to that her remarkable and completely inexplicable knowledge of French cheese, and you would find it hard not to assume that she had been ten years old in the year of the moon landing. But, as I already said, more about that later. Despite all of this, Olga still had the vital naïve sweetness of any normal ten year old girl – just add an incredible mind and an uncanny appreciation for a number of things that were outside of her time.

The only significant flaw in Olga's seemingly-almost-perfect taste, the only blot on that particularly satisfying landscape, was Olga's desire to be woken by Terry Wogan in the mornings, as her radio alarm would shortly reveal. She reasoned that it was completely unacceptable to set it to Radio 1 – the potential for an assault by the aforementioned rappers was too great and too devastating, compared with the possibility of a nice girly pop tune. Any commercial station was likely to seriously offend her by suggesting at eight in the morning that her home could benefit from five dreadful plastic wood-effect windows for the price of four. The fact that Terry Wogan did occasionally flirt with good taste, evidenced by some of the music he selected and seemed to like, just about clinched it.

Olga's dreams were stopped short by the dulcet tones of Mr Wogan and a friendly, if inane, vicar doing their level best to endow the banality of their chat with some semblance of interest and excitement. This morning's drivel was mercifully interrupted by Olga's dad, shouting from the bathroom.

'Come on, darling! Your brekky is ready and the bathroom is free.'

'Okay, Dad. I'm up!' shouted Olga. 'I'll be down in a minute.'

Olga went through the bathroom procedures of teeth-cleaning and face-washing, and quickly put on the school clothes that her mum had prepared for her the night before. She skipped down the stairs two at a time. Olga always felt cosy at this time of day – cosy, and much loved, which she was.

'Hi Mum! Hi Dad!' Olga chirped as she hugged them both.

Olga's mum and dad were absolutely besotted with her, despite her being a very challenging daughter. The breakfast table was a picture of harmony and delight. There was no apparent evidence at all of the serious thoughts that were going through Olga's very capable, but young, mind.

'I've made your favourite sandwiches for your packed lunch, Olga,' said Olga's mum.

'Breast of chicken, with lemon mayonnaise and black grapes?' Olga retorted with glee.

'No, the other favourite.'

'Smoked salmon and brie?'

'Yes. I got some lovely food for the whole week. I went shopping yesterday.'

'Olga, I love you, but you do have the strangest taste for a little girl,' Olga's dad piped up, with a warm smile that said more about how proud he was than how strange Olga was.

As Olga tucked into her breakfast of orange juice and muesli, she chatted about school stuff, and asked about her mum and dad's evening, confirming that their evening was uneventful.

'I'm off now,' said Olga. 'Have a nice day. See you at tea time.'

''Bye, darling,' said Olga's mum and dad – in unison, as always – as Olga went out into the less windy and much brighter day.

On her way to school, Olga's mind was working overtime. So there was no gravity, there were planets all over the place, trees that work like computers, residuals, air that seems to be in charge, and talking things that know everything we forget. Oh, not to mention a cute little alien, a very cute little alien.

Most of Olga's classmates seemed to dislike school. They would rather be playing football, riding their skateboards, or lost in the virtual reality of their computer games. Olga couldn't help feeling that this said more about the way the world was, than about how her classmates were. Generally speaking they were a very likeable bunch of kids.

Olga loved learning. She loved everything about learning, and she loved learning anything at all, even just for the sake of learning. Time between tasks set by her teacher were often taken up on the school computer, fuelled by an insatiable thirst for knowledge, investigating anything and everything. Learning was, however, an area in which even Olga found herself to be a little strange. Things would often crop up that Olga already knew, and she had no reasonable explanation as to why she knew them.

One of these things was her in-depth knowledge of the Apollo moon mission. She was frequently tempted to test herself by looking up facts about this on the internet, only to find inexplicably that there really wasn't much she didn't already know about it. For her own amusement, she quite often looked at the various sites concerning the particular conspiracy theory which suggests with considerable vigour that no such thing as a moon landing occurred. Olga found this laughable; it was almost as if she had been on the mission herself, such was her absolute certainty that it was for real. Olga felt almost as if she had been directly involved in the moon landing at some high level. Of course, she knew this was completely impossible, as it had taken place many years before she was born. The other strange thing about the moon landing thing was that in the very same way that she knew with absolute certainty of its verity, she also knew that it had been a disaster and a catastrophe on an astronomical scale. Olga didn't know why she knew this. All had seemingly gone well on the mission; everyone had returned home safely, but nonetheless she was *certain* of it. In fact she was as sure of this as she was sure that any second now, as she could see from the corner of her eye, Emily was going to say…

'Hi, Olga! Why are you looking at space stuff again? We're supposed to be doing Art.'

'Hi, Emily!' Olga replied warmly.

Emily was about the sweetest and cutest thing in all creation – a little short for ten years old, fragile and delicate in stature and movement. She had the most beautiful round face, the tightest of blonde curls resting delicately on her shoulders and the most vivid bright blue eyes. She always sat with Olga whenever possible and Olga adored her.

'Will you help me finish my painting?' said Emily with irresistible charm 'It's for my mum.'

'Okay, Em. I'll just close this down and I'll be with you.'

'Thanks, Olga,' said Emily smiling.

Olga spent most of the morning helping Emily to create the most wonderful painting to take home to her mum. She was grateful for the distraction; the moon thing had put her in one of her bothered moods. And she couldn't take her mind off speaking with the post on her way home.

Olga needed some answers, she felt inextricably involved in something. Strings were being pulled; she could feel them, and she was going to get some answers. When Olga wanted answers, she usually got them. Olga was the sweetest, loveliest person in the world, but woe betide anyone who messed with her, as many a potential bully had found. No, Olga would not be messed with.

The rest of the school day passed fairly uneventfully. Olga as usual spent most of the day with Emily. Everyone was very excitable on this particular Friday. Fridays were always a bit like that, in that they preceded the weekend, but this particular Friday preceded the Easter holidays, which meant two weeks off school. Olga was normally quite ambivalent about school holidays; she really liked school. This time was different: her famous sixth sense was telling her – no, shouting to her – that spinning out before her was the adventure of a lifetime. The goings-on were so exciting that Olga would gladly have shelved all other projects in her busy life.

That afternoon on her way home from school, Olga came by her normal route – that is, not via the route she had taken this morning. Olga had deliberately avoided the normal route in order to resist the temptation of stopping to talk to the post. That would have been impossible to resist, and she needed plenty of time, time that she wouldn't have had this morning. She was just arriving at the park, and patient as Olga was, even *she* was getting very excited. A small part of her thought maybe she had imagined it all and she would have to endure that face-reddening embarrassment which we all know too well. When we have done something really silly, even though no-one else has noticed, we feel our face getting slightly warmer and redder.

The bigger part of her was sure she hadn't imagined any of it.

Olga arrived at the post and sat down with her back to it, exactly as she had done yesterday. She sat in silence, and was met with the same silence, which went on and on for what seemed like an hour, but was actually about one minute. Olga's heart was pumping as if she had just run a marathon.

Then just as Olga's face was starting to warm, the familiar voice behind her ear said 'Not so windy today, then'.

'What took you so long?' replied an almost out-of-breath Olga.

'Oh! Sorry, my dear, didn't mean to keep you waiting.'

'I thought you weren't going to say anything,' said Olga, still in a bit of a flap.

'Oh, I was just trying to think of something clever to say. I haven't had a meaningful conversation with a person for as long as I can remember. So I didn't really want to start it with "Hi, Olga". I know you people love to talk about the weather, so I thought I would do well to start with that.'

'If it's been as long as you can remember since you have had a conversation with a person, then you have never had one at all.'

'What makes you say that?' the post asked, very slowly and purposefully.

'Because I know that you have infinite memory.'

'Oh dear! Oh deary, deary me! This is getting very serious! How do you know that?'

'Yiptop told me,' Olga retorted, with deliberate mysterious intent.

'And who, pray, is Yiptop?'

'Yes, who is Yiptop?' said a gravelly voice, from just below Olga.

'Don't you start interrupting! Very serious and far-reaching issues are unfolding here. I am perfectly capable of dealing with this without any help from you,' said the post very firmly.

'Oh! Excuse me for living!' said the gravel path, betraying a campness in its voice.

'Can we carry on without you two arguing?' said Olga.

'Yes, of course my dear... So who indeed is Yiptop?'

'Yiptop is my friend. He's from the planet Zog, and he is very clever and has infinite memory.'

'A spaceman!' exclaimed the post.

'A spaceman!' exclaimed the now definitely camp gravel path.

'I won't tell you again! Stop interrupting and leave this to me,' said the post in an authoritative tone.

'He's not a spaceman,' Olga insisted defensively.

'Oh dear me! Oh deary, deary me!' The post said in a woeful and worried tone.

'Why do you keep saying that?' asked Olga, who was now starting to become afflicted with the worries.

'Well, you must be the one. That's the only explanation. It's you – you're the one!' The post was now in as much of a flap as a solid cast iron post was capable of.

'The one what? What are you on about?'

'The one we were told about. The one who hears, the one who could set it right, the one who found the grain.'

'The grain? This is getting very silly.'

'The Grain of Truth. The last Grain of Truth from before the dreadful day.'

'Excuse me! I'm only ten, you know.'

'We were expecting someone older.'

'That's not my fault. You'll still have to explain all this to me.'

'I am sorry, my dear. Although we have been expecting this, it's still a bit of a shock.'

'What is this dreadful day thing?'

'Oh, that was before you were born. 1969.'

'What happened in 1969?'

'You must know, my dear. July 1969. Especially as you have found the grain, the last Grain of Truth.'

'In 1969, on July the twenty first, man landed on the….'

'Don't say it! Don't speak his name!'

'What the…?'

'Stop! Please don't mention his name, we residuals are not to speak of him. Only the great stones, only they can speak of him.'

'If you can't speak of the moo… sorry, of him, how are you going to explain all this to me? If I have a part in all this, I'll need to know what I have to do.'

'Well of course, my dear. I will do all I can. But tell me more of this spaceman.'

'I said he is not a spaceman! Will you stop calling him a spaceman?'

'Oh, very well then. Yiptop.'

'Yiptop started to visit me a couple of months ago. He just appears now and again, and we chat and have fun. He's told me some stuff about the universe and how it really is. He's told me a little about Zog and his family. Oh yes, and he told me to tell you about him.'

'Any more?'

'Yes. He told me that spiders can't get into the bath by climbing up the drain pipe.'

'Oh, can't they? I was sure they could.'

'No, they can't swim or dive.'

'I really think we should stick to the point.'

'And he told me about the trees, and the wind.'

'Did he mention, you know, the… him?'

'No. Well, not really.'

'Well, my dear, it is a sort of *did* or *didn't* thing rather than a *not really* thing.'

'He said his mum was writing a book about the moo…
about him.'

'Oh, well. I suppose that's okay.'

'I think it's time you told me a bit more.'

'I will try and tell you as much as I can.'

'Well, go on then, please.'

'In July 1969 something dreadful happened,
something dreadful and quite catastrophic. Before it
happened, the world was warned that it must not
happen. The warning was ignored and it happened
anyway. It has caused a problem of such catastrophic
proportions that it will likely bring about the end of all
life on this earth.'

'That is what catastrophic means, I guess.'

'Yes, exactly.'

'How exactly does this affect me?'

'Well it affects everyone. End of life means end of
life, for everyone, and for that matter, everything.'

'What am I supposed to do about any of this?'

'I was telling you. You probably know, from your space… sorry your Yiptop, that the balance of this world is very delicately controlled by the trees and the air.'

'Yes, Yiptop explained that to me.'

'You may also know that we residuals play our part by retaining all lost knowledge, until such time as it may be used.'

'I know now.'

'Do you also know that the trees have a web-like sharing system?'

'Yes, like our Internet.'

'Yes. Just don't say that to a tree, my dear. Now where was I? Oh yes – we residuals, by the way, have to pass all our knowledge from pillar to post, so to speak. It can take us a long time, so trees have an easy time.

'There is one more element in this fine balance. That element, which I cannot speak of, is the reason you are here.'

'The moo…'

'Yes. That's right my dear, so you understand then. You are the one – you have you found the Grain of Truth. It will have given you special powers and charged you with the most important job of all.'

'That is…?'

'Well, to save us all, of course. You are the one who can save us all, and what's more, it's going to get urgent now that you are here.'

'Okay, so what do I have to do?'

'Well, the first thing you have to do is go to Salis Bury.'

'Salis Bury?'

'Yes, that's the place – Salis Bury.'

'Where is Salis Bury?'

'Salis Bury, my dear, is the place of the great stones, the great stones of Stonehenge, the greatest of all residuals. It is my job to send you there. My job, after you have been there, will be to do anything you ask me, to help you complete your task.'

'This task?'

'Yes, my dear. This task.'

'You wouldn't like to tell me what this task is, would you?'

'I would love to.'

'Go on, then.'

'I can't.'

'But you said you would love to.'

'I would love to but I would do a very bad job of it, and besides, I'm not allowed to. I am just an ordinary residual. Something as important as this must be dealt with by the great stones. My job is to send you there.'

'No idea as to how I get there, or any suggestions?'

'I am told that the one who has found the Grain of Truth will get there.'

'And that's me.'

'Yes, 'fraid so, my dear. You have the means.'

'I have the means?'

'Yes, that's right. You have the means.'

'Didn't you just say you have to do anything I ask to help me with this task?'

'Yes my dear, but that is after you have been to Salis Bury.'

'I suppose that's it, then. I'll run along to Salis Bury, wherever that is.'

'Yes, my dear, as soon as you can, and come back to see me when you have been. Anything that the great stones ask of you, I will help you with.'

'Thanks for that, then.'

'I will hear from you.'

'Yes. 'Bye.'

Olga got up to leave with a mixture of feelings. On one hand she was filled with trepidation at what she could be facing; on the other hand, excitement at what adventure lay before her. This was one time, she was thinking, that she could really do with a third or fourth hand as well – she had a few thoughts she could put on them, too. Olga stopped walking for a minute. This was one time where thinking and walking weren't working too well together. She felt like she had a huge pile of spaghetti in her hands, with a mass of loose ends, and she had to somehow tie all the ends together. Olga decided it was definitely time for that snug cosy home, Mum and Dad, and her favourite blanket – never more in her young life had she needed that.

CHAPTER FIVE

Olga had rested and had her tea, taking full advantage of her wonderful loving parents in the nicest possible way, and she felt relaxed and rested. It was eight o'clock on this long Friday, and she had said goodnight and gone up to her room. Only Olga knew that the day was far from over, and had very recently become even more complicated, if that was possible.

Her parents had spent most of teatime talking about a surprise holiday that Olga's dad had arranged over the Easter break. For the moment, Olga had no idea how she was going to juggle the visit to Salis Bury, the holiday, and whatever she was supposed to do after Salis Bury.

She was anxiously anticipating Yiptop's knock at the window, in the hope that he would be of help in sorting some of this out. She couldn't help wondering that perhaps she had been naïve in thinking that Yiptop's presence was in any way coincidental, and that he wasn't as inextricably tied up in all this as she seemed to be.

'Hurry up Yiptop, I need you,' Olga said quietly to herself.

'Olga, it's me – Yiptop!' came a voice from the window.

Yiptop's familiar pixie face was again against the window, and what a relief it was for Olga to see him. She got up straight away and opened the window to let him in.

'Ssh! Keep your voice down,' Olga whispered. 'My parents are downstairs.'

'Hi! What's happening? Did you spock to the rissotto?'

'I'll get you a glass of water, Yiptop. Wait there.'

'Thonks. Good I door.'

Olga went off to get some water. Yiptop drank it down in one gulp, as always.

'What's happening, Olga? Did you speak to the residual?'

'Yes! It's all getting very serious. Something to do with 1969, when we sent a manned spaceship to the moon.'

Yiptop was laughing hysterically, as quietly as he could manage.

'Spaceship! That was a pile of scrap metal, about as sophisticated as a washing machine. No-one can understand how it managed to make the journey there and back!'

'Okay, no need to get snobby about it. It did get there and back, didn't it?'

'I guess it did, just about.'

'Anyway, never mind that. According to the residual, it was a very bad idea and we were warned against it by the moon, and it's caused a major problem for the planet, which could result in disaster. And I am apparently the one.'

'Which one is that, Olga?'

'I don't know. How do you expect me to know? He just said I'm the one who's found the Grain of Truth. He said I must go to Salis Bury to see the great stones, and they would tell me all I needed to know and what I must do. He said I am the one who could stop whatever is happening. How am I supposed to get to Salis Bury?'

'No problem. We can go in my LIC.'

'Oh, cool! I'll just pop downstairs and tell my mum that I'm off to Salis Bury in a LIC with my friend from Zog, and that I have to go because the world is all messed up because of the moon landing in 1969,' said Olga sarcastically.

'Yeah, okay… I see what you mean. I'll think of something.'

'While you're thinking, my parents are planning for us all to go on holiday for two weeks and we're leaving on Sunday. That doesn't give us much time.'

Yiptop sat pensively for a few minutes, while all kinds of strange objects materialised in his hands. Olga sat in silence and watched this procedure.

'Right,' said Yiptop, looking satisfied, 'your parents are going on holiday for two weeks. Where?'

'Portugal, and I think they're planning to take me with them.'

'Fine, that's excellent.' He continued the procedure for a few more minutes.

'Okay, sorted, no problem,' said Yiptop, smiling.

'What?' said Olga.

'No problem.'

'What?'

'Is it the *no* or the *problem* that you are having trouble with?'

'Er… both at the moment, especially if they're used together.'

'Okay! Take it easy, and I will explain. We Zoggers are very much more advanced than you. We have many devices, which, with a bit of lateral thinking, can be used to help us. This particular device…'

A pen-like thing appeared in Yiptop's hand.

'..is a memory eraser. It can be programmed to work in a very precise way. If I point it at a person and press this button, it will erase a specific pre-programmed memory. Then the memory will be stored in this device, and can be put back into the person at a later date.'

'Very clever, but I don't quite see how that is going to help us.'

'I'll explain. If I point this at you…'

'Don't point it at me! My memory is fine as it is.'

'Don't worry, it's not activated. But if I were to point it at you, and save you as a specific memory, then point it at me and add me to it, we two will then be saved in it as a specific memory.'

'Yes… then what?'

'Then I point it at your parents, and both you and me will be erased from your parents' memory along with anything directly relating to us. It works very well. The software specifically separates only the memory parameters associated to the initial.' Yiptop went on enthusing about his little gadget in a very boy-like way.

'I think I've just about got the gist of it,' said Olga, 'but do you have to sound so excited about a little gadget? I suppose it's a boy thing.'

'So using this, I can erase you and me from your parents' memory. They will go off quite happily on holiday, without you or any memory of you, and without the memory of seeing me pointing this at

them. That gives us two weeks to sort all this out.'

'You're mad! Forget it. Think of something else.'

'What's your problem? It's a perfectly good solution.'

'This is my mum and dad we're talking about! I'm not

letting you mess with their heads with your alien

gadget. What if something goes wrong?'

'It already has – with your world, and we are supposed

to try and fix it.'

'Think of something else, something that doesn't

include messing with my mum and dad's heads.'

'Olga, calm down! Nothing will go wrong. If the

device gets lost or broken, it will have already backed

up its memory in the nearest residual. The nearest

residual is this house. I can get these so easily, I could

get another one. It's fool proof.'

'Well, I'm still not sure about all this, and while we're

on the subject of being sure of things, I'm sure you

know a lot more about all this than you're letting on.'

'That's crazy.'

'Not, I know you do. There's no way that you just

turned up at my house, and then just a couple of weeks

later all this stuff starts to happen around us.'

'I am not supposed to interfere,' said Yiptop looking a

little uncomfortable.

'It's a bit late for that now.'

'I'll tell you all I know.'

'Everything?'

'Everything.'

'Go on, then, and we'll see where we go from here.'

'When I was on a trip to Earth, just to have some fun.

Something very strange showed up on my LIC sensors

– two things, actually. One, zero moon radiation,

moon radiation is absolutely essential on a mooned

planet, only mooned planets sustain life, there is no air on non mooned planets. Two, I was picking up a small amount of moon radiation from the planet itself, only a very tiny trace, but moon radiation only comes from moons, it never comes from the planet.

'What does moon radiation do?' asked Olga, getting very intrigued.

'Moon radiation governs the other elements on the planet – the air, the trees, and the residuals. It also has a moderating effect on some of man's more aggressive and selfish traits. Most importantly, it provides the facility for people to use creativity, and really that's the only thing that substantially separates them from everything else. Without, it the planet runs wild. There is no balance, no creation, nothing new. So I followed this trace of moon radiation and found the source of it.'

'And where was that?'

'Here. *You* are the source. The moon radiation is coming from you.'

'Me!'

'Yes, you.'

'How me?'

'I don't know how, it just is.'

'Great! Now I'm a moon!'

'Not quite.'

'Well, it looks like I'm the nearest we have to one at the moment.'

'So, anyway I had to find out what was going on. I'm not supposed to interfere, but this was a situation that shouldn't exist, and a very big problem.'

'So I'm giving off moon radiation. Why?'

'I don't know. I said I would tell you all I know, and that is all I know.'

'What will happen to us without all this moon radiation?'

'I don't know. It doesn't happen. Air does not form on planets without moons. So there is nothing to go on. This just shouldn't happen.'

'But it has!'

'Yes, and do you remember I told you that people didn't achieve interplanetary travel until they had also attained a level certain level of wisdom?'

'Yes, I remember that.'

'Well, part of that wisdom would tell you that you don't ever land on moons. The other part would tell you that you don't travel to other planets till you've sorted out most of the major problems on your own planet – but that is what I think you call a catch twenty two.'

'And we did, in July 1969.'

'Yes, very crudely and who knows how, with a pile of washing machine technology.'

'And here we are with a problem.'

'Yes, and that's why I'm here. I am hoping that I might be able to help. Also I feel a strange sort of calling, which tells me I must help.'

'But is it too late?'

'I honestly don't know. If there is an answer, it lies in the moon radiation that's coming from you, and whatever the great stone residuals have to say.'

'Then we have to go to Salis Bury to find out.'

'Okay. We'll have to use the memory pen thing.'

'Good,' said Yiptop, looking very pleased with himself.

'When shall we go, then?' said Olga, sounding a little more cheerful.

'We should go to the stones at night. For one thing there are always too many people around at daytime. I have flown over there before, and two young people wandering about talking to the stones will attract a bit of attention, and we don't want that.'

'Tomorrow night, then.'

'No, we've no time to waste. We need to go as soon as possible. Aren't you worried Olga?'

'No, if you can do something, do it, if you can't, don't worry.'

CHAPTER SIX

The park was very bleak at night. The wind had started up again, and though not as strong as it had been lately, it was trying to be.

The post was enjoying its usual pastime, and job, of listening to all that goes on around. This is how the residuals got a lot of their information. The other way was linked directly to people's memories. In the process of transferring information from short term to long term memory, an electro-magnetic radiation can be detected. It is this radiation which carries any lost or forgotten information to the residuals.

Residuals have a kind of hierarchy and are very like individuals, with their own separate consciousness. The hierarchy is based on age combined with exposure to knowledge, so the older and more knowledgeable the residual, the higher its position over others. The issue of what is and what isn't a residual is a fairly complex affair. For example, a residual old iron anvil might be melted down and recast into an iron post, continuing its original consciousness. On the other hand, certain materials will lose their consciousness when transformed. The particular scientific process is complex and subject to much variation. Usually, stone retains consciousness for the longest, particularly if it stands apart from other stones. Sometimes if it is joined for a long period of time with other stones, it will enter into a shared consciousness with them. When large stone residuals are split, the largest part retains consciousness and the new part may restart anew.

The greatest and most powerful residuals on the planet were the stones of Stonehenge. This is not because they are the oldest stones; it is the combination of their age and their continued exposure to information that makes them the greatest. Information is passed in a linear way from residual to residual, unlike with trees, which have their web of interconnection.

The post, meanwhile, was continually chatting away to other residuals around him and keeping them informed. There was a real fever in the vibes, an almost tangible excitement. Since 1969, known throughout the planet as *that terrible year*, there had been an atmosphere of sadness and apathy. In the previous years, the world, the air, the trees and the residuals had enjoyed a feeling of hope and happiness, and had felt confident in the reasonable certainty of continuation, which, whatever was said by human philosophers, was actually what it was all about. Now, since the revelations surrounding Olga, things were buzzing with hope – not certainty, but hope. Not certainty, because Olga was a last hope, a real hope, but no-one knew what she would achieve, only that it was possible that much could now be achieved to set things right. The residuals were abuzz with speculation.

Abuzz with speculation, and at the same time doing their jobs, performing their function with renewed diligence. Watching and listening more thoroughly than ever. In this watching and listening, and despite the renewed hope, residuals were realising just how far things had slipped away during this moonless period. It was almost as if they had been afraid to look too closely, in fear of what they would have seen.

The post was listening to four teenagers who were gathered around it. They were regulars, and often congregated there. As usual they were drinking from several cans of beer, and getting more and more excitable as the evening progressed.

Kyle was the biggest and noisiest of the four. Not too bright, he was typically obsessed with the physical and material, an increasingly prevalent trait in humans since new generations with new, creative ideas of their own seemed to have disappeared.

'So, what we doin' then? If you lotta babies are too scared to nick it, I gotta do it as usual,' said Kyle in a mocking tone.

'I ain't no baby,' said Arnie. 'I nicked one last mumf, an' I'll be doin bird for 'at. They got my prints now, 'avun they? 'Swy I'm wearin' these stupid gloves, innit?' said Arnie, who was wearing a pair of pink washing up gloves.

'I thought you was goin' 'ome to 'elp ya mummy with the washin up!' said Kyle jabbing him in the ribs, and laughing at him.

A sort of pathetic mock-sparring session ensued between Kyle and Arnie with the others geeing them on.

'Wha' 'bout you, Del? I ain't 'eard you say nuffin.'

'Yeah, well I ain't tooled up, am I? I ain't gonna be nickin' no car wivout no tools, am I?' said Del defensively.

'I got 'nuf tools to 'ave any car, so that's no problem, is it?' said Kyle, challenging Del to the task.

'Right, I'll do it then, but if I nicks it, I'm drivin' it – that's the rules, innit? When Arnie nicked that Merc, 'e drove it, din' 'e?'

'Yeah, an' I was too drunk to see where I was goin' – nearly ended the misery for that old codger an' 'is missus!' laughed Arnie.

'Yeah,' said John, always the quietest, and never too keen to participate in any skulduggery. A born coward, too scared to start anything, too scared to stop anything. John would go along with anything, and be the first to run when it got tough. There were people like John in all walks of life.

'Right then, use my tools, but I'm 'avin' the Bee Em and drivin' it. You can 'ave that Rover in front of it, an we'll 'ave a race five times round the park, an' see who can drive,' said Kyle, who was up for a challenge today. He had far too much latent energy and aggression, and needed to burn it off.

'Right,' said Arnie, 'that's sorted. 'Oo's got the beer, then? 'Sno point nickin' 'em till afta midnight, 'cause there's too many people about. All we'll get is aggro. Might as well 'ave a drink, innit.'

'I got more,' John piped up, holding four more cans in his hands. John was pleased that the plan for the evening had evolved without any risk on his part. John's intention was to monitor the race from the sidelines, if possible, and not actually ride in any of the cars, if he could get away with it. The post was listening to this, and thinking about it. Yes, residuals could think – rather better than some people, they were beginning to realise. Who could blame them, when you consider that what was going on that night was pretty well par for the course. The post knew, of course, that no-one would be listening to him, but nevertheless he felt he should say something.

'So it's Brands Hatch again, is it? Who are you going to kill today? You people are growing with no souls, and there are more and more of you. You respect nothing and no-one, not even yourselves.'

The gang were drinking more beer and generally behaving more abusively and aggressively to passers by. John was drinking very little. He was playing his usual trick of pretending to drink as much as all the others, while remaining more or less sober, for his own protection. It wasn't that John was in any way a more noble or caring person than the others. John was simply a bigger coward.

Midnight came, and by now, it was clearly evident that the boys had drunk far more than they could cope with. Except for John, who, although the others hadn't realised it, had drunk only a half can of beer.

'Come on then, get the cars. I wanna see 'oo's gonna win this race,' said John, doing his best to gee them on.

The park was about a mile long, with dual carriageways running the length of both sides, and joined up by roads at each end of the park. One of the roads was met at the corner of the park by another main road; this junction was governed by a set of traffic lights. These lights were about twenty yards from the post.

'We'll get the cars and warm 'em up, then we'll start at the lights, proper Formula One style, then five times round the park. First past the lights on the last lap wins,' said Kyle, always the self-appointed leader.

''Oo's got the job of standing by the lights to see 'oo's first across the line?' said John.

'You said it!' said Kyle laughing.

'Yeah! 'Sabout all you're good for,' added Arnie.

'Why's it always gotta be me?' said John, pretending that this wasn't exactly what he wanted,

''Cause it is, right?' said Kyle, squaring up to John in his usual bullying manner.

'Right,' said John. 'It's the last time, though.'

John was inwardly very relieved at securing what he believed to be the safest position.

John and Arnie hung around by the post, while Kyle and Del went off to the other end of the park to steal the two cars they had selected.

Kyle and Del were not the brightest of people by any means. Somehow, though, they had learned sufficient to steal cars with remarkable ease.

They knew, for example, that the older BMW had pneumatic locks, which could easily be opened by placing a sink plunger over the lock and pressing firmly. They also knew, and were equipped to deal with, the more modern locking system of the Rover. Entering the cars took about fifteen seconds. Then an eighteen-inch length of scaffolding made swift work of both steering locks, freeing the steering wheels, and giving easy access to the wiring and alarm system. Within five minutes they had possession of both cars and were warming up the engines.

Emily was sitting in what she called her princess seat, in the back of her dad's car. She liked this seat; it lifted her high enough to see everything that was going on, and it felt safe and comfortable. Emily had been out for the evening with her parents, having dinner with her aunt and uncle. Her parents let her stay up late on occasions like this, when there was no school the next day. They'd all had a lovely evening. Emily's mum was proudly holding a beautiful painting that Emily had made for her at school. She had insisted on taking it with them, to show everyone how good it was. Emily and her dad were singing along to a CD of music from his younger days on the car's CD player. The song, 'American Pie', was a favourite of Emily's about the day the music died. Music and singing, along with painting, were the things that made Emily most happy.

There was by now a dampness in the air, that kind of wetness which sort of hung in the air, like the very finest of rain, that didn't seem to actually fall, it just sort of hung.

Del was sitting in the Rover and grinning maliciously at Kyle. He had by now realised that chance had given him the more powerful of the cars.

Kyle wound down the electric window of the BMW and shouted to Del, 'You got no chance in that, sucker!'

'We'll see 'bout that, big boy!' shouted a confident Del.

'Twice round the park to warm up, then we start at the lights!' shouted Kyle.

They went off to warm up the cars, the damp road eliminating any tyre squeal.

Kyle and Del's experience with cars was limited to how to steal them and how to make them go. Capable drivers they were not. When combined with cars, their confidence and arrogance were a potentially fatal mix for them and for anyone around them.

The two cars arrived at the start line, and Arnie jumped in with Del to join the fun, leaving John standing by the lights. The red light was joined by amber as they revved their engines, ready for the immediate left turn at the start. Red and amber disappeared, to be replaced by green. And they were off. Del tucked away a good start, his front-wheel-drive car pulling itself round and into the first short straight. Kyle spun the rear wheels uselessly on the damp road, wasting valuable time and losing several seconds, which put him ten yards behind Del. The next turn arrived quickly and Del lost some advantage by braking too early. Kyle braked later, and took a wide line sweeping in to the turn. He was now right on Del's back bumper. Del's superior power soon had him gaining ground down the long straight and there was now some space between them, as Del noted in his rear view mirror. As Del approached the next turn he began to brake sharply in preparation. Kyle saw this as his only chance. He too had now realised that the Rover was the more powerful car. Kyle left his braking even later this time, and flew past Del, taking the Rover's door mirror as he passed. He reached the bend having dropped a gear, and put his foot down hard. The rear-driven wheels spun out, lining the car up for the new short straight. Kyle was now firmly in the lead and needed to retain it for the next bend. His disadvantage would be on the long straights. They more or less held their positions for the next three laps, saving the real battle for the last lap.

John was jumping around with excitement at the lights. The flat park allowed him an unimpeded view of the whole race.

Emily and her parents were just coming towards the junction at the park as Kyle and Del were finishing their penultimate lap. Both Kyle and Del were determined to gain the advantage for the last lap and were heading to the lights at the highest speed so far. They arrived at the lights neck and neck, just as Emily's car was crossing the lights. Both cars hit Emily's car at about the same time, driving it sideways into a stone wall the other side of the lights. Six airbags inflated in a nanosecond massively increasing the pressure in the car, and cosseting all the occupants like cotton wool. Emily heard a loud bang, then silence, accompanied by a searing pain in her ears. The pain would be a long time subsiding, and it was going to take her parents a long time to adjust to living with Emily in her now-silent world. The rapid pressure increase had catastrophically and irreparably ruptured both her eardrums.

The car that had been following Emily's clipped the rear end of Kyle's BMW, sending it spinning back towards the park, where a shocked John was watching, rooted to the spot. Before he could move, the BMW hit him, breaking both his legs at the knee, the car's underside crushing his head. There was not enough time to feel any pain. Just nothing.

As the BMW continued to spin, it hit the post and ripped it from its concrete foundation. Kyle's head impacted with the windscreen. He had no time for a last thought. The light went out, never to come back on.

Surprisingly, the Rover was relatively undamaged, as were its occupants, Del and Arnie.

Chance plays no favourites, not in this world.

CHAPTER SEVEN

'So when are we going, then?' asked Olga.

'I think we should wait till your parents are asleep, and while they're sleeping, I'll erase us from their memory,' said Yiptop.

'If you do that while they're sleeping, you'll only need to erase me, because they won't have seen you.'

'It's better if I erase my potential image as well. That way, when I put you back, they won't even see me – it will be as if I didn't exist.'

'Cool! That means you can visit me any time and they won't see you. I've always wanted an invisible friend!'

'It's nearly nine o'clock now. What time are they usually asleep?'

'How would I know?' Olga replied, surprised that he had asked.

'They're your parents!'

'Yes, but I'm ten years old, so I'm always asleep before them. They get up around seven o'clock, and I guess people need about eight hours' sleep – so, eleven o'clock, maybe?'

'Okay. Then the best idea is that you sleep now, for the few hours we have at least.'

'Okay, then. Goodnight.' Olga lay down on her bed – then sat back up again immediately.

'Are you crazy, Yiptop? How am I going to sleep now? I'm just about to take a ride in an alien LIC – see? I didn't say spaceship – all the way to Salis Bury, wherever that is, to have an important meeting with some very big stones, to try and work out how we can save the world. And you think I can sleep!'

'You Earth people need sleep! Whatever is going on is very important for the whole planet. So you, being a very important part of it, need to be on top form. The only way you're going to be on top form is if you get some sleep.'

'I agree. You're right,' said Olga and closed her eyes.

'I'm not asleep yet!' she said a few seconds later, giggling with a mixture of excitement and over-tiredness.

Yiptop saw the funny side and giggled along with her.

'Look at my face,' he said.

Olga looked at his face, and his eyes seemed to glow. They glowed with a warm penetrating colour she had never seen before. Within a few seconds, she slumped on the bed and was fast asleep.

Zoggers like Yiptop didn't need sleep. They did, however, benefit from rest, so he lay on the floor for a while till it was time to wake Olga.

Yiptop was not quite as unflappable as he liked to appear. He knew that he needed to be strong to see Olga through this. He also knew that this was not likely to be all fun and games. He didn't know how things would turn out or what would be expected of them. Yiptop would never start anything without finishing it, nor would he shrink from a duty he had taken on. He knew that it was his duty to guide and protect Olga through all of this. He just didn't quite know why he knew this.

The time was now one in the morning. Yiptop had allowed Olga as much time as possible to sleep, and enough time for her parents to fall into a deep sleep. He looked intensely at Olga, focusing directly on her closed eyes. Olga sat bolt upright, in one movement.

'I'm looking at your eyes, so what's supposed to happen? Are you going to hypnotise me or something? I've never been hypnotised. This will be fun!' said Olga.

'Look at your watch,' said Yiptop, looking very pleased with himself.

'It's one o'clock! That's impossible! What happened?'

'You've been asleep for four hours. It should be enough – hypnotic sleep is very restful.'

'I've been hypnotised?'

'Yep!'

'And I missed it! I can't believe I missed it.'

'Everyone who is hypnotised misses it. If you don't miss it, it's because you haven't been hypnotised,' said Yiptop, matter of factly.

'That's no fun. I thought being hypnotised would be fun. Well, never mind. My dad always says life's full of disappointments.'

Yiptop began to look restless. 'We need to get into action. There is a lot to do. It will take at least a half hour to get to Salis Bury.'

'Okay, what do we do first?' asked Olga, readily conceding the lead role to Yiptop.

'You go quietly into your parents' room and check they are asleep, and while you're pissing the bathroom, you'd better get me…'

'A gliss of waiter?' said Olga, delighted to score a point.

'Yes thanks!'

Olga tiptoed to her parents' room and quietly opened the door. She could see they were fast asleep, and whispered, 'Love you! I'll be back soon – I really have to do this, sorry.'

Olga stopped by the bathroom to get Yiptop a glass of water.

'There's your waiter!' said Olga, chuckling. 'My mum and dad are fast asleep.'

'Good, I've scanned me into the memcap. Now you,' said Yiptop, pointing the pen-like device at Olga.

'Can't feel anything. Is it working?'

'Of course it is. I told you it wouldn't hurt. Now I have to scan everything in the house, so I can eliminate anything connected to you.'

They both went all around the house until Yiptop was satisfied that he had covered everything.

'Just one thing,' said Olga. 'When my parents come back, and you put me back in their heads, they'll remember that they've been on holiday without me. Won't they find that odd?'

'Oh! I hadn't thought of that!' said Yiptop in mock surprise. 'What are we going to do?'

'Come on then, clever clogs, what are we going to do?'

'Simple! The memcap will reattach you to their current imagined holiday, which it has recorded, and you will be slotted into all the relevant places.'

'One day I'll think of something you haven't, you'll see!'

'I'll go and zap your parents, then.'

Olga led Yiptop to her parents' room and he pointed the memcap at them for a few seconds, then they quietly shut the door and went back to Olga's room.

'Now,' said Yiptop, 'I have a permanent water supply in the LIC. You will need food.'

'What about food for you?'

'Zoggers don't eat. Didn't I tell you that?'

'What, never?'

'No.'

'Not even something really yummy like smoked salmon?'

'No, we evolved out of eating about a million years ago.'

'I love eating!'

'I know, so we need to go to your kitchen.' A blue oval object, about the size of a tennis ball, appeared in Yiptop's hand. 'Then I need to point this at all the food you like.'

Olga had to say something this time.

'Where do all these things keep coming from?'

'What things?'

'You know – like that,' said Olga, pointing to the blue oval thing in Yiptop's hand.

'Oh, that. From the LIC.'

'Like, they just jump out of the LIC, fly through the walls and land in your hand, without a word?'

'Yes. How did you know?' said Yiptop.

'Never mind,' said Olga, wishing she had resisted mentioning it.

'The food, then.'

'Yiptop, sorry to keep asking questions, but why do you want to point that at the food?'

'Because you need to eat.'

'And…?'

'This is attached to my LIC replicator.'

'And who is your LIC replicator?'

'It's a device that will replicate things. That is, if I point it at a hamburger, then you can get hamburgers whenever you want.'

'Yiptop, if you point that anywhere near a hamburger, I will never speak to you again!'

'Relax! I will point it at all the food in the kitchen, and you will be able to eat what you like from the LIC replicator.'

'Okay. This is a lot to take on board, you know.'

'I know, and you are doing very well.'

Yiptop meticulously scanned every food item in the kitchen, taking care not to go near anything that resembled a hamburger, then they went back upstairs to Olga's room.

'Right, that's all done. Get everything you need, and we can go.'

Olga put her coat on, picked up her favourite teddy bear and looked around the room for anything else she might need.

'Ready,' said Olga.

'We'll leave by the back door downstairs, then.'

They went downstairs, and out through the back door, into the garden, down to the bottom of the garden, where the shed was.

As they passed the shed, Olga was expecting to see a sort of flat, modern-looking, flying-saucer-type thing, or a flashy sort of pointed rocket-type thing. She would actually have been happy with any-type thing. But what she saw was no-type thing at all.

'Where is it, then?' asked Olga in disbelief.

'It's here. Don't worry, just stand next to me.'

Olga stood right next to Yiptop, as he had asked. Suddenly but slowly, and quite smoothly, they both started to rise into the air.

'No, stop! I don't like this! Where's the spaceship? You didn't say we'd have to fly! I don't do flying!' said Olga in panic.

'Take it easy and trust me,' said Yiptop, in such a calm voice that it did calm Olga down, but only a bit.

'Okay, I'm calming down! Can we go down now?' said Olga. 'Where's the LIC?'

'We are in the LIC. You can sit down and walk around. It's quite safe,' said Yiptop, completely failing to pacify Olga.

'Yiptop, this may be fine for you, wandering about on air, but I'm not going to get used to this. We'll have to find another way to get to Salis Bury.'

'Hold on, then. I'll try to morph some visuals.'

'Just do something, quickly please! Or get us down!
We're still going up at the moment.'

Yiptop's screen appeared in front of him, and he
concentrated on it for a minute. Suddenly the environment
changed.

'Right... So now we're flying in the cupboard under
my kitchen sink! Is that the best you can do?'

'Hang on. I'll try something else.'

'If it's a straight choice between hanging in the Air a
thousand feet up, in nothing, or my kitchen cupboard,
I'll go for the cupboard.'

Yiptop concentrated on his screen a bit more. In an
instant, they were in Olga's bedroom.

'Fine now, we're back home, I don't know how you
managed that, but it's much better. Shall we just get
the train to Salis bury, like anyone else would?' said
Olga, a little exasperated.

'No,' said Yiptop reassuringly, 'we're still in the LIC. It's just morphed into a replica of your bedroom.'

Olga walked around it quite confident that this was actually was her bedroom. She opened the door and jumped back about two yards, went down on her hands and knees and crawled back to the door.

'Yiptop! My bedroom's flying! How's my bedroom flying? Where's the rest of my house?' she said nervously.

'No, your bedroom is still in your house. This is a morphed replica. I'll save these settings. I think you will be more comfortable travelling this way. No-one else can see it.'

'Okay, this is cool. I can handle this,' said Olga, getting her breath back. 'How do you fly it? Where are the controls and things?'

'All the controls are mental.'

'If you ask me, Yiptop, the whole thing is mental!' said Olga, now relaxed enough to laugh.

'We will be in Salis Bury in about twenty minutes. May as well relax and have something to eat till then. What would you like?'

'I would love a breast of chicken sandwich with lemon mayonnaise and black grapes, please.'

'Hold out your hands,' said Yiptop smiling.

As Olga held out her hands, a plate from her kitchen appeared, with exactly what Olga had ordered on it. Possessing remarkable recuperative capacities, Olga was munching happily through her sandwich in minutes.

They were now gliding smoothly over the landscape towards Salisbury, Olga was enjoying the view through her bedroom window, and wandering what the next surprise might be.

CHAPTER EIGHT

'See that?' said Yiptop, looking through the window with Olga.

'Yeah! Wow!' Olga replied, looking down at the big stone circle about five hundred feet below them.

'It's the stones. We need to land somewhere. I'll find a quiet field not too far away,' said Yiptop, drinking from a large glass of water which had appeared in his hand.

'Yiptop, you have to teach me how to do this making-things-appear trick. It's so cool!'

'It's not a trick. It's the LIC that does it. But unless you want to wait a couple of million years to evolve the right brain structure, you won't be able to give the instructions.'

'Okay, guess I'll have to rely on you then. Any chance of orange juice?'

'Hold your hand out.'

A large glass of orange juice with ice, appeared in Olga's hand and she drank it.

There was a slight bump, just about the slightest bump you could possibly imagine feeling.

'We've landed,' said Yiptop as his view screen appeared in his hands. 'We are about five minutes' walk from the stones. Grab what you need and I'll de-visualise the LIC and we'll make our way over to them.'

Olga put on her coat and looked at her old teddy bear, which was on her bed. Just then a thought occurred to her.

'Yiptop, I've had my teddy bear since I was born. Can a teddy bear be a residual? Do you think it could speak to me?'

'It's perfectly possible.'

'It would be so great. He'd remember everything I've forgotten, and that's loads. I've spoken to him since I could talk, but he's never answered.'

'Bring him with you. Maybe something will happen. This is the most powerful residual on the planet, so you never know what might happen.'

Olga put on her coat and tucked her old teddy bear under her arm. Olga and Yiptop suddenly found themselves standing in an open field.

'I'll never get used to this disappear-reappear stuff,' said Olga.

'You just have to keep in mind that *visual* is just one small part of perception, and probably one of the smallest parts at that. Things don't exist or not exist by virtue of weather you see them or not. Many more things exist that you *don't* see, than exist that you *do* see. Even those things that you perceive by touching are only as you perceive them, because of their particle order. You can take a simple object like a cup.'

A yellow cup appeared in Yiptop's hand. 'Change the particle order and you have…'

A pair of pink wellington boots replaced the cup.

'Yiptop, I'm only ten. I'm doing my best, but this is all a bit beyond me.'

'I think you understand much more than you realise.'

'Maybe, but why the pink wellies?'

'Because we have a bit of walking to do and you will get your socks wet with no shoes on.'

'I had slippers on a minute ago.'

'Yes, and now they are a pair of pink wellies, see?'

'Cool! I'll put them on, then.'

'Right. Let's go find the stones. Are you ready for this?'

'After the last few days I think I'm ready for anything,' said Olga smiling.

The intrepid, if unlikely, pair, wandered off across the field, looking every bit as strange as they were. Yiptop looked like a 1930s schoolboy in his slightly too long short trousers. Olga walked next to him in pink wellies, with her teddy bear tucked under her arm.

I doubt that anyone who saw them walking across the field that night could ever have imagined that these two were the last hope for the survival of a possibly doomed planet. They crossed a brow and in front of them lay the most majestic vista that little Olga had ever seen.

'Look!' said Olga. 'It's them, it's the stones! Wow! They're awesome.'

'Yes, they look important,' said Yiptop, not wanting to look too impressed.

'Yes, you're right, they look important!'

'They are the most important residuals on the planet, so I guess they would have to look important.'

They approached the stones and sat in the centre of the stone circle. The sound of the stones surrounded them, but the voice was somehow less deep and intimidating than Olga had expected.

'Greetings, Olga and the spaceman,' said the stones.

'He's not a spaceman,' said Olga, remarkably defiant in the face of such great authority.

'Oh! I am sorry if I offend my, dear. Greetings, Olga and Yiptop from Zog,' the stones said, clearly keen to be correct.

'How do you know I'm from Zog?' asked Yiptop, curious.

'We have seen your people before now, and respect you greatly. Welcome, friend!' replied the stones.

'Thank you,' said Yiptop. 'I acknowledge and return your respect.'

'Yes, me too,' said Olga, keen to participate in the preliminary diplomacy.

'I know why you are here, and I will tell you all I can of what must be done. I know that there may be much that you know already, but to ensure your full understanding I will start at the beginning. Yiptop, your memory is much like ours – you will forget nothing of this, I know. You have come this far, so can I assume you are pledged to take this to its conclusion?'

'I am a Zogger.'

'And that means?'

'That means that once started, something must be finished. We hold this sacred. It is fundamental to our being.'

'Your people on Zog, do they know anything of this?'

'No.'

'Then excuse me for asking, but you are young. Will they not seek you when you fail to return after some time?'

'I am young, but I have reached the age of commitment.'

'Meaning?'

'Meaning that as I have sent a message to the effect that I have started something, they will understand and will not expect me to return until it is completed. They will not interfere without my request.'

Yiptop was thinking that if they actually knew that he was trying to save a very primitive planet, they would go ballistic, but as Zoggers they still wouldn't actually interfere.

'Then I can only trust and hope that your ability to help matches your obvious enthusiasm and commitment,' said the stones.

'I will do all I can,' said Yiptop solemnly.

'First, my dear Olga, I must tell you something about the world, about the universe. This planet is to the infinite universe, with its infinite planets, as a grain of sand is to a beach. As unique as the moon itself is the

126

last Grain of Truth given to you by the moon. All planets have limited life, the span of which is not one split second in an immeasurable eternity. For life to transcend that eternity there is one great importance over all things – that is continuance. At the top of the pyramid of the order of things is the greatness you will know as the gods. Whatever you may call them, and however great the reverence with which you worship them, matters not. They are too distant from us in every way. Other than to follow their chain of knowing, we need have little concern for them other than to know they exist.

'This chain of knowing comes to us through time, from the development of people, with the interaction of all things sentient.

'The spiritual continuance of people beyond their physical life is a direct matter for the gods. It is no longer more than marginally dimensionally attached to anything within this universe. The proper order of development on this planet is a matter for the moon. The moon monitors and guides the development of life on this planet within the proper order of things. The air takes heed only of the moon's wishes. Little interference occurs in this process – that is, until a great wrong, which may threaten continuance in the universe, transpires.

'Understanding all of this will be of great difficulty for one so young. If not for the timely intervention of our friend from Zog, it would have been necessary that you spend some considerable time in my company, but we are fortunate that we can rely on Yiptop and his infinite memory to keep you informed.

'As I have said, the only serious threat to the universe is that which threatens continuance. Continuance on a single planet is of negligible import compared with the continuance of the universe. In the proper order of things, the moon and the Air have a greater duty to the universe than to an individual planet. Where a threat is posed to the universe, by an individual planet, they would be obliged to neutralise either the threat or the planet. Sadly they have very limited means by which they can eliminate the threat. There are few things on a planetary level which would be considered a threat to the universe. One of these things is the attainment of interplanetary travel. This cannot be allowed to take place until a level of understanding has been reached whereby such evils as greed and the insatiable desire for power have been eliminated from people's primitive being. It is rare that such off-planet excursions occur, but sadly it happened on this planet in 1969, during an ongoing battle fought in the name of greed and control between two nations of this planet.

'Rather than any attempts to resolve differences and use resources to improve life for the whole planet, or just have a war as usual, this race for supremacy was begun. This became a race, of all things, to reach the moon, with no purpose other than to get there, it seemed. It ended with a primitive, and all but impossible, landing upon the moon. The moon knew this was coming, and some time before the event, it implemented the only course of action available within the proper order of things. It issued, in June of that year, a warning of a nature so subtle that it was sadly understood by no-one. You may well ask why it was so subtle as to be missed. That is because it is the responsibility of people to conduct their lives, and interference by the moon must be limited and delivered only in the most extreme cases. When such interference is deemed necessary, it must be done in such a way as to leave responsibility with the people, and not take it away. The purpose of the moon is to regulate extremes, and engender creativity in mankind, not to run the lives of people.

'This warning arrived in the form of a popular music song. At the time, this was considered to be the most common communication form among the most enlightened. This song was called 'Something in the Air', and was performed by Thunderclap Newman. This of course is only of passing interest, as the warning did no good, I'm sorry to say, despite the song becoming a classic of its genre. As the warning was issued and ignored, and the landing still took place, the moon now has only one further option available in the proper order of things, before the Air must leave the planet to perish, and attach itself to another mooned planet, fulfilling its duty to the universe. That option is where you come in, my dear. I am sorry to have rambled on. Do you have any questions so far, being so young?'

'I think I understand most of what you have said. Me and Yiptop can go through it later, anyway,' replied a very concentrated Olga.

'Good. Then I will go on,' said the equally concentrated stones.

Yiptop remained silent and serious while the stones continued.

'The moon allowed itself this one further interference. A seed was sent from the moon to earth, containing the last Grain of Truth – the entire wisdom and truth of life. It was hoped that someone would find this seed, which possessed properties designed to make the finder desire to eat it, thereby instilling in that person the gradually growing wisdom and truth of all life. The moon then sent a message to the Spirit of Moondog, the Spirit of Leprechaun, and to the Air.'

Olga looked very puzzled at this part, and the stones noticed this.

'I can see that this confuses you, my dear. For many years in the history of life on this planet, there were other occupants. They became extinct when their purpose expired. These other occupants had direct spiritual links with the great gods of all dimensions. They were in various forms – Leprechauns and Moondogs, and there were also Elves and Wood-nymphs, which you will know perhaps as Fairies. These demi-god creatures were linked directly to the great gods themselves. The great gods don't continue direct links after a certain stage in development, and when that stage was reached, these demi-gods left the planet. However the presence of the spirit of such beings is continued and passed down for all time. So there exists but one dog who is the Spirit of Moondog, one man who is the Spirit of Leprechaun, and so on.

When they die, the spirit lives on in one of their offspring. So it was that the message was sent to the Spirit of Leprechaun and the Spirit of Moondog. It said that one who holds the last Grain of Truth will come, and when that person comes, they must assist in every way so that their great and important work should be done. When it is time, the Spirit of Leprechaun will recognise you and will know the whole story, and the Spirit of Moondog will obey your every command, and when all is done, he will relay all the information to the moon – only Moondogs can speak directly to the moon. Having completed these options, the moon then stopped all influence on this planet, other than the necessary physical work of maintaining oceanic stability. This shutdown will continue until the moon is satisfied that a safe future is assured. So now we come to the great task which you must carry out.'

Olga and Yiptop sat completely captivated by the almost hypnotic voice of the stones, which seemed to be coming from all around them.

'You must travel from here back to your hometown, where you must find the Spirit of Moondog. There will be one dog in your town who will be alerted by the name Prudence. When you find this dog, you must say *dear Prudence, won't you come out to play.* The dog will acknowledge you; any of its associated people will forget its existence, and it will follow you on your great journey. In fact the Spirit of Moondog will be with you for all your life and the lives of your children after you. You must then go to a place called Whitehaven. When you get to Whitehaven, you will be met by the Spirit of Leprechaun. He will take you on a great journey across the frozen seas of the far north, near the frozen land of Knud Ramussen. There you will travel still further northwards until you are met by the Air, at its most powerful centre of communication, in the place known as the Domain of the Air. There you will have an audience with the Air, and certain things will be asked of you. Do you understand, my dear?'

'Do I have any choice in all of this?'

'My dear, choice is a much-talked about concept in people. Truly I think you know that, as no-one makes the choice to be born in the first place. Furthermore, no choice can be made as to the circumstance of birth. Choice therefore is not even relevant. This is your destiny as if born to it. We must all do what we must do. The fate of this planet is in your hands. Can you choose to ignore it?'

'You're right. I have no choice. I'll do my best.'

'No more can be asked of anyone or anything.'

Olga and Yiptop began to emerge from what seemed like an almost trance-like meditative state. It was Olga who then spoke first.

'So let's see if I've got this right. We get back in the LIC, go home, find this dog called Prudence, go and see the post as promised, back in the LIC, off to Whitehaven, find the Leprechaun, then take him with us in the LIC to some frozen place... Yiptop will remember the details!'

'One more thing,' the stones interjected. 'Once you leave the confines of this land, you must travel with the Spirit of Leprechaun by the means he provides.'

'Okay, and what happens when we get to the Air? What will he want?'

'You must ask the Air that, my dear. Go now and prepare yourself for this great journey, and for the life you will then lead as the bearer of the Grain of Truth. One day, I think quite soon, you will realise that although you are charged with an enormous responsibility, you also have the great privilege of sharing your life with all other sentients on your planet, playing a part in the great universal truth. You will also serve gods themselves.

'Farewell for now, my dear Olga, and all thanks to you, Yiptop, our friend from Zog. May your deeds receive the protection worthy of their greatness.'

'Thank you,' said Olga. 'I'll let you know when it dawns on me how privileged I am!'

'Thank you,' said Yiptop.

The two wandered back towards the LIC in silence. Not a word was spoken between them until they were in flight.

CHAPTER NINE

Yiptop was drinking his customary glass of water while Olga was eating another sandwich.

'Yiptop, you will remember all of that, won't you?' said Olga.

'Of course! I don't forget anything – you know that.'

'So I don't need to try, then.'

'No, but I'm sure you will remember most of it anyway.'

'Probably, but my brain's a bit fried right now.'

'It is a lot to deal with. Why don't we talk about it later? We need to chill for a while and let it all sink in,' Yiptop said.

'Yes, I think you're right. So what do we do next?'

'Well, we should stay away from your house for a while. Your parents aren't going away on holiday till tomorrow night, so we can't do anything very useful there.'

'Shouldn't we start looking for this dog straight away? We have lots to do.'

'I don't think we can be wandering about at night looking for a dog. Daylight is only a couple of hours away. Have you ever watched a sunrise?'

'Yes, I've got up early a few times and watched the sun come up.'

'But have you watched it from space?'

'Not that I remember, but right now if someone told me I had, I would probably believe them.'

'I don't think you have, so let's go into orbit and watch half the planet gradually going from dark to light!'

The LIC stopped its smooth forward movement and started a much more dynamic upward motion.

'I can go much faster as the Air gets thinner,' said Yiptop. 'It's the Air that keeps the speed down on-planet. Once in space it's a different matter entirely. I can get home to Zog, in only a little more time than it took us to get to Salis Bury."

'Don't get technical, Yiptop! I'm a girl, and girls understand technical just as well as you. We just don't feel the need to be quite so absorbed by it.'

'Look!'

Olga looked through the window, to see the Earth they were gradually leaving. It was becoming a globe, just like the one they had in school. She could see clearly the oceans and land masses.

As they rose higher, Olga became conscious of a shift of awareness. She'd had these before, the sort of shift of awareness after which nothing seems quite the same anymore. Olga began to realise that the *more* they went up, the *less* up it became. *Up* sort of shifted into *away*, and lost all of its upness. At an unknown point, a point which seemed to be indefinable, *up* simply became *away*. Once they got far enough away from Earth, there was no up and down – it had been replaced by near and far. Olga's mind, during all she was going through, was becoming more and more refined. She was now starting to cross-conceptualise, taking physical concepts like relativity, and making comparisons with philosophical concepts.

Olga was thinking, if *up* stops being *up* at a certain point, then maybe other things stop being whatever they are, the more they are.

'Yiptop, the higher you get, *up* stops being *up*, and it becomes *away*.'

'Yes,' said Yiptop, wondering quite where this would go.

'So does everything change?'

'How do you mean?'

'Well, I think I know what I mean, but I'm not really sure I know how to say it.'

'I think what you might mean is, everything exists only within its finite conceptual parameters.'

'That could very easily be what I mean, if I knew what that meant.'

'It's not the easiest thing to explain. In fact, it's one of the hardest things to explain, but I'll try. When we use words like *big*, *small*, *more*, or *less*, they are relative terms, which means they can only actually exist within a comparative frame. *Up* can only have any relevance, if there is a *down* to compare with it. The further *up* goes away from *down*, the more its relevance diminishes, until it exceeds its conceptual parameters, and can't exist anymore.'

'Yes, I've got that, but does that apply to everything?'

'How do you mean, everything?'

'I mean that the more you have of something – even if that something is just, say, a nice feeling – it must also become less, the farther it goes away from its comparative opposite.'

'I see.'

'Like you can't get happy, and just keep getting happier.'

'No, just look at happy as up, and sad as down, separate them too much and neither of them have any meaning. They will have exceeded their conceptual parameters; they don't have absolute values – their values depend on the existence of a comparative opposite.'

'Good, now I understand something about conceptual parameters.'

'One of the problems with primitive civilisations, such as you have on Earth, is that there is no universal grasp of conceptual parameters. People try to isolate themselves from other people's problems and misery in the belief that they will be happier.. Actually the reverse is the truth.'

'I've heard people say less is more.'

'That's kind of true. Where people really get in a mess is with material possessions. They get into a sort of spiral. They want, so they obtain, then they find they still want, so they obtain more. They don't stop and think, hey wait a minute here, I wanted and I obtained then I wanted again and obtained again, and now I still want, this isn't working. That's why you have millionaires, and people starving.'

'If only the millionaires realised how much comparative happiness they could enjoy by living in a world closely related to people who are starving, sharing to improve their position.'

'True, but that isn't only because of not understanding conceptual parameters, it's partly not having the courage to take a step that isn't directly rewarded by a primeval system of brain chemistry reward.'

'Now you've lost me.'

'Don't worry! We won't solve the basic problems of mankind in one conversation. As you go through life you will gradually learn all of these things and much more. You have been gifted with the Grain of Truth by the moon, so your mind will develop very quickly. For now, try to remember this. Knowing is the first step to enlightenment, the next is understanding, and after that comes the will and courage to transcend your natural instincts, and choose the way you live.'

They looked through the window and watched a line between dark and light very slowly moving across the Earth, bringing night and day at the same time.

'That is a sunrise!' said Yiptop, proudly.

'Cool!' said Olga. 'In one motion it gives the Earth its opposites of day and night!'

Tired, Olga started to yawn and fell asleep there and then on the floor by the window. Yiptop picked her up and put her on her bed, and placed her teddy bear next to her.

He then set a course for the park, and soon after they landed behind the building next to the post.

'Wake up, Olga!' said Yiptop, gently.

'I must have fallen asleep. Can I have a glass of milk, please?' a bleary-eyed Olga replied.

A glass of milk appeared in Yiptop's hand, and he passed it to Olga.

'Thanks,' said Olga, drinking the milk.

'We are at the park. When you're ready, we can go and speak to the post.'

Olga got up to look through the window. 'Are you sure people can't see my bedroom, plonked here at the park?' said Olga, still a bit sleepy.

'No, I told you, no-one else on Earth can see it. All they could ever see is us appearing and disappearing. I only de-visualise it for general neatness.'

'That's better!' said Olga, finishing her milk. 'Let's go and see the post.'

Olga left the LIC first, and ran around the corner towards the post.

'Yiptop! Yiptop, quick!' Olga shouted in shock.

'What's happened? The post has gone!'

Yiptop ran after her.

'Where was the post, Olga?' Yiptop said, in a calming voice.

'Here! Where this hole is! It's gone! What's happened?'

'Look at all this broken glass. It looks like there's been some kind of car accident.'

'Over here, my dear! I'm over here!' came a voice from a doorway.

Olga and Yiptop ran over.

'I'm down here,' said the post.

The post was lying on the floor just inside a porch.

'What happened? Are you okay?' said Olga, very concerned.

'Oh, I'm fine, my dear. Don't worry about me. It was dreadful, those poor boys!'

'What boys? What happened?' Olga asked.

'Oh, hello spaceman! Nice to meet you at last,' said the post. Olga let it go this time.

'The boys that hang around here in the evenings. They stole two cars and were racing around the park. They had a terrible accident. Two of them died. It was quite horrible. A dear young girl in another car passing by was hurt as well, but I don't think she was hurt very badly.'

'That's awful! They must have crashed into you,' said Olga.

'Oh, they knocked me right out of the ground! Don't worry, though. Someone will put me back in the next few days. I'll be fine. But never mind me – tell me about *your* adventures.'

Olga and Yiptop sat down in the porch next to the post.

'We've been to see the stones,' said Olga.

'Oh, I know! All the residuals have been talking about it. The stones were very impressed and the vibe is very optimistic.'

'So you know all about it already? Then you know what we have to do.'

'Oh yes, and you will have the support of every residual on Earth.'

'That's nice. And what about the trees?' Olga asked tentatively.

'Oh! The trees… great thinkers the trees are, but I wouldn't expect too much in practical terms. Not too good on the practical side, the trees, not the greatest doers.'

'But will they help?'

'Oh, I'm sure they would *want* to help, but the only real help you can get from the trees is when you need some thinking done. Great thinkers.'

'What about something like where do we find this dog?' Yiptop interjected.

'They may well help with that. That's a thinking problem, and they know the ways of him. Problem is, they're not great communicators, that is except with each other. They rarely speak to anyone or anything. Talking to trees is a bit of an experience,' said the Post.

'I'm about to speak to one, so a bit of advice would be nice,' said Olga.

'Well, the main thing to remember is that the trees already know just about everything worth knowing. So by now, they will already know exactly what you are going to ask them.'

'How?'

'Well, by now they will know what you know, they will also therefore know what you don't know, so they will deduce what you need to know, and expect you to ask that. Also they speak very fast. And you will be very privileged indeed if the tree enters into any idle chat at all – even one word of it.'

'That's all very well, the tree knowing what I will ask, but will it know the answer?' said Olga.

'Probably, but stand well back if it doesn't. Trees don't like not knowing things.'

'Do they get nasty?'

'Oh! Goodness me no, they just get very embarrassed, and can lose a few leaves, even the odd branch, but it's quite rare. Basically a tree will stick to the point, expect you to understand first time, and then stop. I would be surprised if the whole conversation took more than a minute or two.'

'Okay, should I choose any particular tree?'

'Oh, yes. A small one.'

'Why is that?'

'Fewer and lighter branches to fall on you,' advised the post.

'Okay.'

Olga looked around and pointed at a very small tree about fifty yards away.

'Yiptop,' she said, 'shall we talk to that little tree over there?'

'Okay, let's go for it,' said Yiptop.

'See you in a minute then, post,' said Olga, as they walked off towards the tree.

'Hello, tree!' said Olga, brightly.

The tree answered immediately in a voice that sounded almost exactly as you would expect a packet of crisps to speak, that is, if you ever did expect a packet of crisps to speak.

'Well, you see, it's a moon thing, and moon things are never obvious. In fact they are so never obvious that they are completely obvious. The moon would hide a book on a bookshelf – the last place you would look for a hidden book. The first place I would look, if I knew the moon had hidden it. Obvious dog to you, small, friendly dog, living with nice friendly people. So, look for big nasty scruffy dog, living in bad conditions with horrible people. Scruffiest biggest nastiest guard dog you can find, that will be the dog. You'll find it.'

'Thank you, tree. Er… can't be more specific, can you?' said Olga.

'More specific? More specific? Shall I uproot and walk you to the dog? Maybe bring a lead, and shout "walkies!"?'

'Okay, sorry! Keep your leaves on! We'll find the dog.'

'Not an Internet user, are you…'? Oh, never mind.'

'Tree, why are you so grumpy?'

'Grumpy? Grumpy! I'm not grumpy – *busy* is what I am. Lots of thinking to do. No time to chat. Far too much thinking to do. 'Bye.'

Olga and Yiptop went back to the post.

'That was certainly an experience,' said Olga.

'Yes, that was an experience,' said Yiptop.

'Oh, that's trees for you,' said the post. 'Do you think you can find that dog now?

'I don't have the faintest idea, to be frank,' said Yiptop.

'I do,' said Olga. 'There are some scrap yards on the outskirts of town near the canal. They have huge guard dogs and they don't look after them properly. They're always angry. I think we should try there first.'

'Good thinking, Olga,' said Yiptop.

'You had better go off and look for the dog, then,' said the post.

'We'll go now, shall we?' said Olga.

'Yes, let's go,' said Yiptop. 'See you later, post.'

'Yes. 'Bye for now,' said the post, as they both headed off to the LIC.

'Trees are very strange,' said Olga.

'Yes, though I expected as much,' Yiptop replied.

'Are they like that on Zog?'

'Pretty much, I guess. We don't speak to them often these days.'

They got back in the LIC and took off towards the canals. Olga guided Yiptop to a field, very near to the scrap yards.

'Yiptop,' said Olga.

'Yes?'

'You know how you can make things appear, when you need them?'

'Yes.'

'If we're going to be wandering about looking for a dog, do you think it might be better if you were dressed in a way that sort of blended in a bit better?'

'I am dressed like a school boy of my age.'

'Yes, but from some history book. Nobody dresses like that any more.'

'What would you suggest, Olga?'

'Maybe like this.'

Olga had picked up a magazine with a picture of a skateboarding teenager in it, and showed it to Yiptop.

'I can dress exactly like that if you like,' said Yiptop.

'It's not a matter of whether I like it. It's more about blending in.'

'Okay, done!'

In an instant Yiptop was dressed exactly like the skateboarder in the magazine.

'Much better!' said Olga.

They landed, got out of the LIC and wandered off towards the yards.

'I can't believe we'll be lucky enough to find the dog this easily,' Olga said.

'Maybe we will. The tree seemed quite sure he had got it right,' Yiptop replied.

They walked on, and got to a closed-up scrap yard. In the yard was a large bulldog. Olga and Yiptop went right up to the chicken-wire fence.

'Prudence! Come on, Prudence!' shouted Olga.

The bulldog ran at an amazing pace towards the fence and launched himself at them with terrifying aggression. When he landed back on his feet he just stood there, growling and glaring at them.

'Not him, perhaps,' said Olga.

'I don't think so,' said Yiptop.

They backed off and went on to the next fence. Sat in a corner, chewing on a bone that was bigger than most dogs, lay a big brown and white dog – the biggest dog Olga had ever seen. It looked a bit miserable and bedraggled, and frankly disinterested.

'What about him?' said Olga.

'Bit big,' said Yiptop.

'Yes, it's a St Bernard,' said Olga. 'They're used for mountain rescue.'

'Try it,' said Yiptop.

'Prudence! Come on, Prudence!' said Olga.

The dog got up on its feet and abandoned its bone. It didn't run but walked very positively towards them, and sat, as if to attention, by the fence.

'This could be the one,' said Yiptop.

'Ssh!' said Olga, concentrating on the dog.

'Dear Prudence, won't you come out to play?' said Olga quietly.

The great big dog purposefully got back on all fours, turned away from them and started walking away.

'Not this one, then,' said Olga.

'Wait, look!' said Yiptop.

The dog had walked as far away as possible, and was now running at full lolopping speed towards them. As the dog got within a few yards of the fence it leapt, so high it was almost as if it was flying. It completely cleared the fence, landing at their side of it.

Yiptop and Olga found this a little disturbing. They were very much hoping this was the right dog. The dog got within two yards of them and sat to attention.

'I think this is the dog!' said Olga, excited.

'Talk to it. It's supposed to obey you if it's the right dog,' said Yiptop.

'Prudence! Come and sit beside me, please,' said

Olga.

Prudence walked over to Olga's side and sat, awaiting

the next command.

CHAPTER TEN

'We've got the dog, then! That wasn't too difficult,' said Yiptop.

'Thanks to the tree. Strange things, trees, aren't they?' said Olga.

'Very. We need to get Prudence cleaned up and fed – she's a bit smelly.'

'How are we going to do that?'

'We'll get back to the LIC and go somewhere quiet. I'm sure I can sort out some way of cleaning her up… it is a her, isn't it?'

'Of course she is!' said Olga, indignant at the very idea that Prudence would be anything but.

Olga turned to Prudence and said, 'Follow me and stay close. We're going to get you cleaned up and fed.'

Prudence looked as pleased as fourteen stone of St Bernard could look, as she dutifully followed Olga, a couple of inches from her side.

'I've always wanted a dog! She's beautiful, isn't she?'

'I'm sure she's a very special dog, Olga!' Yiptop replied with a smile.

The three of them got back in the LIC, and took off to an isolated field just outside town. Yiptop materialised a shower of water and some kind of shampoo. Within about half an hour, Prudence had been transformed into the most beautiful, clean, and sweet-smelling St Bernard you could ever imagine. Her brown and pure white coat was shining and soft.

Olga and Yiptop sat down, and Prudence sprawled out next to Olga's bed, looking very happy, having just eaten what Yiptop had prescribed as being a perfectly balanced diet.

It was now Saturday lunchtime, and so much had happened in the past few days. As she ate her lunch, Olga quietly reflected over all the things that had gone on and the way they were all connected. She was becoming more and more aware of the way her mind was subtly altering, in particular the way she was able to reason and correlate information. An uncanny maturity was developing within Olga's mind and she was keen to understand it.

'Yiptop! You made a mistake, didn't you? Are you going to tell me about it, or shall I tell you?'

'Why do either? We both know what it is.'

'True, so the question is, how are we going to sneak back into my house?'

'Yes. We need to get your real teddy bear instead of the replicated one, so that we can try to get it to tell you exactly what happened with the Grain of Truth.'

'Very good, Yiptop!' said Olga, delighted to have been ahead for once, although she was fairly sure that Yiptop had probably realised this before she had.

'Yiptop, how did that happen? What about your infinite memory?'

'Having infinite memory is not the same as being infallible. While busy with other things, it is perfectly possible that I could fail to recognise, and include, a particular element, even though it is in my memory.'

'In other words, you forgot!' said Olga, smiling and determined to take full advantage of this revelation.

'No, I didn't forget, I just failed to include one fact in the equation.'

'Because you forgot!'

'No, I didn't forget. It was in my memory all along.'

'Okay,' said Olga, deciding to let it go for now, 'so we need to sneak in and get him.'

'No, we don't. I can transport him here. I'll do it now,' said Yiptop, a bit ruffled.

Yiptop's screen appeared and he got to work on it. Olga's replicated teddy, disappeared from her bed and a minute or two later an identical teddy reappeared. Olga went over to the bed and picked up teddy.

'Hi teddy, so this is really you?' said Olga, not actually expecting a reply.

'Yes, it is me, Olga! Where have you been?'

'That's a long story! But how come you're speaking to me now?'

'I don't know really. I just couldn't find the words before. I was trying to speak all along. It just sort of never got through!'

'Cool, I've got an invisible friend, seen a real sunrise, got the best dog ever, and a talking teddy bear, and I'm about to go on the greatest adventure of my life, as if I'm not already in it! It's not even my birthday!

How much better and more exciting can it get? Teddy, what do you know about me eating some grain from the moon?'

'Olga! You can't speak his name to me! I am only a residual.'

ff

'Oh, yes – the grain. One day when you were about eight or nine months old, it was a sunny day and you were crawling around in the garden, dragging me behind you by the ear as usual. You saw something glowing brightly under a bush. Being Olga, you had to investigate it. You picked it up, went into a sort of trance, and proceeded to swallow it. I don't think you've been the same since, but not in a bad way. Once you had taken the grain, you became *more* of all the good things you already were. You became kinder, more loving, more intelligent, and much more perceptive. It's just grown and grown since then and seems to be growing even faster now!'

'So it was that long ago?'

'Oh, yes. It goes back to the time I still had fur,' said teddy.

'Are you up-to-date on all that's happening, teddy?' Olga enquired.

'Just about – but who's that lying on the floor?' said teddy, almost in a whisper.

'That's Prudence. She'll be with us for always now.'

'Spirit of Moondog?'

'That's right.'

'A bit big, isn't she? Friendly, though, I hope.'

'Yes, she's lovely and very friendly.'

'Good! Wouldn't want something that big being unfriendly.'

'I don't think we should hang around any longer. We need to get on,' said Yiptop.

'We said we'd go back and see the post. I was thinking, Yiptop, that seeing as he started all this as far as my involvement's concerned, it might be useful if he could come with us. It wouldn't be difficult, now he's not fixed in the ground.'

'I don't see why not,' Yiptop replied. 'We can ask what it thinks.'

'Shall we do that, then?'

'Okay. But there is another little problem – there is more than one Whitehaven. Which one should we go to, Olga?' said Yiptop in the most teasing voice he could manage, and clearly trying to recover from his previous embarrassment.

'You know which one. The one nearest to the northern oceans,' Olga replied with a confident grin.

'Okay, well done! That's the one. It's in Cumbria.'

This was now formulating into quite the most unlikely group imaginable. They were all off to see if a cast-iron post wanted to join them on their journey, before completing the group by adding the Spirit of Leprechaun. Olga wasn't thinking 'how strange is this?' On the contrary, she was having the very best time, in company more suitable than she'd ever had in her life. She had been far too busy to miss her parents or Emily.

They landed near the park, in a quiet little corner hidden by some trees.

'Right,' said Yiptop. 'There are a lot more people about here, so we need to be a lot more careful going in and out of the LIC, because it just looks as if we appear and disappear. Trust me, it can really freak people out. That's why I tried to land somewhere slightly more discreet, not far from the post.'

They walked across the park to the doorway where the post was in temporary residence.

'Prudence, you need some exercise,' said Olga.

Prudence was sitting dutifully, looking at Olga, ready to obey without question and with pleasure.

'I think you should run a few laps of the park while we talk to the post,' Olga, said pointing across the park.

Prudence galloped off, leaving Yiptop and Olga at the doorway.

'Hi, post!' said Olga.

'Oh, hello both. Was that dog the... er...?'

'Spirit of Moondog,' said Yiptop.

'Oh, good, good! You'll be off soon, then.'

'Yes,' said Olga. 'Come with us, post! You'd enjoy an adventure. The experience would stay with you forever,' she added, doing her best to sell the idea.

'Well, there is no reason why I shouldn't. But first, you must agree that if I become a burden, you must leave me wherever that may be,' said the post in seriousness.

'We'll all return safely,' said Olga.

'That is always the expectation when people embark upon an adventure. History will show you, however, that such expectations are frequently over-optimistic. I shall not come without the assurance that you will not allow anyone to suffer for me. Also that you will not allow me to hinder the successful outcome of the expedition.'

'If those are the terms, we should respect them. What do you think, Olga?' said Yiptop.

'I think it is very easy to *say*, but will be much harder to *do* if the situation arises,' Olga replied, with her usual honesty.

'I'm sorry,' said the post, 'but I would need your assurance on that, Olga.'

'If that's what you need, I will respect your wishes, then,' said a resigned Olga.

'So that's settled, then,' said Yiptop. 'You, me, the post, and Prudence.'

'I would like to come too, if that's possible,' said the teddy's little voice from under Olga's arm.

'Yes, of course you can come,' said Olga. 'That will be okay, won't it, Yiptop?'

'Fine with me.'

'How are we going to transport you, post?' Olga enquired.

'Hang on. I'll sort something,' said Yiptop, fiddling around with his view-screen.

Just then a skateboard and a ball of string appeared next to the post.

'We'll get him on this skateboard and tie him on. He'll be easier to move around.' Yiptop looked pleased with himself.

'Good idea,' said Olga.

They secured the post to the skateboard and started back to the LIC.

'Prudence! Come on, we're off!' Olga shouted.

With startling alacrity, Prudence returned from her romp around the park and headed directly for Olga, and took up her now usual place right next to her.

Back in the LIC, Yiptop had a large glass of water. Prudence had an even larger drink of water, and Olga had another sandwich.

They lifted off for a gentle flight to Whitehaven. Yiptop estimated that the journey should take about two to three hours and suggested that upon arrival they could all do with a rest. The search for Spirit of Leprechaun would be better left to the next morning.

'Are you sure it's a good idea to wait till tomorrow? We still don't know how long the next journey will take us,' said Olga.

'I see your point, but I don't think we can consider such an expedition, which is likely to be very tough and dangerous, without being at our best for it. The only way to be at our best is to get the rest we need,' replied Yiptop in his best authoritative tone.

'I think he is right, my dear,' agreed the post. 'We really should conserve ourselves for the long game.'

This being settled, they continued their journey. Everyone and everything rested in their own way. Olga and Prudence were the only ones who actually slept, being the only ones who did sleeping.

They soon arrived in Whitehaven and Yiptop found a place near the coast to set down the LIC. He decided to let everyone continue resting till morning.

CHAPTER ELEVEN

It was eight in the morning. Olga had slept well and woke up refreshed and hungry.

'Morning, Prudence!' Olga said, hugging the huge dog who was becoming her closest companion.

'Morning, Olga!' said the other travellers.

'Any chance of breakfast, Yiptop?' asked Olga.

'Sure! What do you want?'

'Grapefruit and milk, if possible.'

Two halves of grapefruit and a large glass of milk appeared in front of Olga and she tucked into it.

'That was really yummy,' said Olga, finishing the last drop of milk. 'What about Prudence?'

'She ate just before you woke up,' Yiptop replied.

Prudence's head was turning back and forth each time Olga or Yiptop spoke. She seemed to be following the whole conversation. If Olga spoke directly to her, her head would move from side to side, as if extending an ear to her and concentrating on every word.

'So, Yiptop, how are we going to find Spirit of Leprechaun, then?' asked Olga.

'Woof!' came a deep, gruff sound from Prudence.

'I'm not really sure,' said Yiptop, more or less ignoring Prudence's bark.

'Woof! Woof!' barked Prudence, a little louder this time.

'What's the matter, Prudence?' said Olga, stroking her to calm her.

Prudence put her heavy paw up to Olga and gave a whine.

'Is it the Spirit of Leprechaun that's bothering you?'

'Woof, woof, woof!' replied Prudence, still pawing at Olga.

'Do you think you know where to find him?'

'Woof!' replied Prudence with a short bark which could only be interpreted as a very definite yes.

'If she thinks she can find him, then that's not only the best lead we have, but right now it's the only lead we have,' said Yiptop, who had been carefully observing Prudence, while all this was going on.

'Should we let Prudence take the lead and follow her?' asked Olga.

'I don't have a better idea. Why don't we go out and see what happens?'

The three of them left the LIC and ventured off towards the town.

Whitehaven was a seafaring town. You could smell it everywhere. This part of the Cumbrian coast had a great seafaring tradition. Unlike the great ports of Britain which provided passage to the Americas or Europe, the Cumbrian ports gave access to Ireland, the Hebrides, and the frozen waters of the north, into the arctic, Iceland and Greenland. It was home to some of the toughest and most resilient seagoing people – brave, relentless, rugged, and capable of navigating some of the most treacherous areas on the planet, areas that were navigable only for short periods each year. Areas that endured both the midnight sun and the long, endless night – the end of the world, the frozen magnetic north, the uninhabitable ice cap. The home of the Air.

As they arrived in the town, Prudence led them to the seafront. Laying at anchor, a motley selection of battered old fishing boats littered the harbour. Prudence stopped at a visual vantagepoint and sat facing the sea. She raised her head and let out a shocking deep bass howl, a howl that could not be bettered for carrying power by the greatest of foghorns.

'Prudence, what's the matter?' said Olga, alarmed. Prudence turned to face her and lifted her paw in a calming gesture, which both Olga and Yiptop understood, and read as 'don't worry'. She let out another howl of the same pitch and volume, then another – three in all. Prudence turned to Olga and Yiptop and let out a deep but gentle bark.

'I think she's telling us to wait,' said Olga.

'Okay, we'll wait,' said Yiptop resignedly.

They waited patiently for about twenty minutes.

'Maybe we should walk about a bit,' said Yiptop eventually.

'Maybe,' said Olga. 'Nothing seems to be happening here.'

They started to walk a little way, but Prudence didn't move.

'Come on, Prudence!' said Olga.

But still she didn't move. As Olga and Yiptop turned to walk further away, Prudence ran up to Olga and gently took hold of her sleeve in her mouth. She pulled so that Olga went back with her to where they had been standing earlier. Yiptop followed along.

'I suppose we wait some more,' said Yiptop.

'Okay, Prudence. We'll wait till you're happy to move.'

As they were waiting, they watched the boats in the harbour. There was some activity on one of the boats. It was too far away to see much detail, but clearly someone was lowering a small tender into the water.

'Yiptop, is that a very small boat, or a very big man?' Olga asked.

'Hard to tell from here,' Yiptop replied, as he materialised his view-screen. Then, looking at the screen, he said, 'It's a very small boat and a very big man.'

'You'd expect a big man to invest in a bigger boat,' said Olga, amused at the spectacle.

'True, but not everything is as we expect.'

'You can say that again!' said Olga, chuckling.

They both sat down next to Prudence and waited. As they looked along the seafront road, they saw nothing except a few figures in the distance. All was now quiet in the harbour, just the sound of the gulls and the clanking of the boats' hardware.

Suddenly Prudence pricked her ears up. It seemed she had heard something. She was making those excited whimpering noises that dogs make when they are expecting something. She was looking down the road, and her head was moving from side to side, as it did when Olga was speaking to her. She seemed to be looking at the people in the distance and sniffing the air. Her tail started to wag frantically and she began to pant. Just then, Olga and Yiptop heard a sharp high-pitched whistle. The source of this whistle was an enormous bearded man in the distance. Prudence ran as fast as she could towards him and jumped up into his open arms. The man was so big that even Prudence's enormous bulk was dwarfed by him as he wrapped his arms around her and carried her like a small lapdog towards Olga and Yiptop. As he drew nearer, Olga estimated him to be considerably more than seven feet tall, with huge broad shoulders.

He had a mop of dark brown hair and a full dark brown beard. He put Prudence down and she ran back towards them, excitedly taking her place at Olga's side.

'I don't know what you think, but that's no Leprechaun,' said Olga to Yiptop.

'I don't know about Leprechauns, but he's coming this way, and Prudence seems to know him,' replied Yiptop.

The huge giant stood in front of them, all but plunging them into darkness. A huge smile appeared on his face, a smile that took his face over, a smile that could take the world over. Olga had never seen a smile like that. It said, 'I bring only love and I will protect you with my life.' The smile had already said more about the man than a million words could tell. Olga and Yiptop were spellbound and speechless all at the same time.

'I am Sionan,' said the deepest, strongest voice Olga had ever heard, in a strong Irish brogue. A voice with such depth and vibration that Olga would not have been surprised if nearby buildings had crumbled and fallen to the ground.

'So it's all true,' said Sionan. 'You have come, Angel of the Moon and Spirit of Moondog. I feel the moon in the Air again, and see it in your eyes.' He held his arms out wide. 'Come to me, my child. I am Spirit of Leprechaun.'

He swept Olga up in his arms and hugged her with a gentleness that only the strongest people know, then set her down again next to Prudence. He put his giant hand on Yiptop's shoulder.

'Thank you, spaceman. Thank you for bringing the Angel of the Moon to me, and thank you for all you have done and will do for this world.'

'Oh, don't mention it,' said Yiptop, unused to such openly-expressed gratitude.

'My child, I have waited long for this day,' said Sionan.

'I was expecting someone smaller,' Olga replied meekly, in one of those moments when she really wished she'd thought a bit more before speaking.

'I can understand that' said Sionan, his heavy brogue showing through the depth of his powerful voice.

'Leprechauns have always been known as the little people, but I am not a true leprechaun. I am custodian of the Spirit of Leprechaun.'

'We could go back to the LIC and make some plans,' said Yiptop tentatively.

'Sure, young spaceman, but would you indulge me by telling me what a LIC is when it's at home?'

'When it's at home, it's a small green thing, about the size of a tennis ball,' Yiptop replied.

'Sure, you're dead set on confusing me now, spaceman.'

'*When it's at home* is just a saying, Yiptop, he just wants to know what a LIC is,' Olga interjected, seeing the funny side.

'Oh, sorry,' said Yiptop. 'It's my vehicle.'

'Sure that would be very nice. Would you be having any food in this vehicle? All this is making me very hungry.'

'Of course. Anything you want,' said Yiptop, at last getting a bit more comfortable.

'I'll warn you, I take some feeding,' Sionan said, smiling that infectious smile.

They walked back to the LIC, Sionan holding Olga's hand, his other hand on Yiptop's shoulder, with Prudence now dwarfed by the giant trotting alongside.

'You called me Angel of the Moon,' said Olga.

'Sure that's what you are, my child. Did no-one tell you that?'

'No.'

'My child, when you took the Grain of Truth, you became the Angel of the Moon. You carry the spirit of the moon itself, just as I am Spirit of Leprechaun.'

'But you can still call me Olga.'

'Sure I will call you Olga.'

'While we're on names, Yiptop prefers to be called Yiptop. He's not really a spaceman, he's from Zog.'

'So we've got that all sorted then – Yiptop, Olga, and Spirit of Moondog.'

'She's called Prudence,' said Olga.

'Sure Prudence it is, then.'

They arrived at the LIC, which materialised around them.

'So you fly around in your bedrooms, where you come from?' said a very amused Sionan, ducking to fit under the ceiling.

'No,' said Yiptop, 'I can make it take any form. This was to make Olga more comfortable.'

'That's good magic! Is it difficult to do?' Sionan enquired.

'No, it takes a few seconds,' said a proud Yiptop.

'Well then, could you make the ceiling just a bit higher, so then I could stand up?'

Yiptop adjusted the ceiling, adding about two feet for Sionan's comfort.

'So where's the kitchen, then?' asked the hungry giant.

'There's no kitchen,' Yiptop replied, 'but tell me what you want, and I'll sort it out.'

'Could you manage an Irish breakfast? That's eggs, bacon, sausage, tomato, mushrooms, fried potatoes and black pudding.'

Yiptop was looking at his view-screen. 'I can't do black pudding, but all the rest is okay.'

'Sure that's very nice, but if that's some kind of space age microwave oven, I'll not want to cause any offence, but I'll be off to the little café in the town.'

'No, don't worry, Sionan,' said Olga defensively. 'It's not a microwave. Yiptop replicates food from my kitchen. It's always yummy.'

'What will you have to drink with that?' asked Yiptop.

'A pint of Guinness would set me up for the day, but I doubt you could replicate that. The English have been trying for a long time!'

'Yes, Guinness is on the menu! Keep still.'

A tray appeared on Sionan's lap containing all he had asked for.

'Yiptop, you'll make someone a wonderful wife one day!' said Sionan.

'I can't make people,' said Yiptop, missing the joke completely, as Olga and Sionan laughed.

Yiptop provided food for Olga and Prudence and as they all ate and chatted, the conversation came around to the more serious issues that had brought this unlikely team together.

'How much do you know?' asked Sionan.

Olga and Yiptop updated Sionan on all they knew and all that had happened so far.

'What happens next is your part,' Olga concluded.

'I have to tell you that so far, my friends, your quest has been easy. We have before us what can only be described as a dangerous and arduous journey, even with yours truly as expedition captain. There is but one accepted route by which a traveller can reach audience with the Air. That route is by sea to the northwest coast of Greenland opposite Elsmere, via the Davis Strait and Baffin Bay.

'At this time of year the journey is barely possible. For most of the year the journey is impossible, and at no time is it easy. It is a long journey, and even with my vast experience and knowledge of this ice bound region, the attempt will take not less than twelve days. I say attempt, because no such journey can ever be described as anything but an attempt. At the end of the sea journey, if we have the fortune to survive, we will trek across the frozen land coasting the Lincoln Sea, north of Knud Ramussen Land, northwards till the Air has the mercy to accept us.

'You will please understand one thing. It is the responsibility bestowed upon me to captain this journey. My word will be final on this mission, from the minute we leave these shores, until the Air accepts us. There is more. There is no guarantee that we will complete this journey, and no guarantee that we will any of us return. Angel, you, sadly, have no choice, like myself and Prudence. Our world is doomed by the action of our people in a matter that threatens universal continuance, against the proper order of things. Should we fail in this mission, or choose not to undertake it, we will perish in any case. You are young to bear such responsibility, but the cards are dealt, and all we can do is play them. Yiptop, you can leave now with your life. This is not your battle, you have helped us so far, and we are grateful.'

'But I am a Zogger!' said Yiptop with pride.

'And that means…?' Sionan replied.

'That means that once started, things must be finished.'

'Upon that principle, you would stake your life?'

'That principle *is* my life; without it, I am nothing. So you see, Sionan, I have no more choice than you.'

Sionan hugged Yiptop, in the way he had hugged Olga. She was sure she saw tears in his eyes, as he said, emotionally,

'May the Gods bless you for your honour and strength, may we thank the Gods for bringing you to us, our great friend from Zog, sure you could be that saving of all of us.'

Listening to all of this, Olga felt more and more the moon inside her, as she spoke in a trance-like state: 'The end calls, and in calling, offers the chance of continuance if we follow the path of truth. If we walk away, the end will seek us and find us. In walking away, we will have proved the case for the end. In approaching the end we prove the case for continuance. These are the words of the moon.'

They all listened in silence.

'Did I say that?' said Olga, out of her trance.

'The moon gets stronger within you. You will become accustomed, my Angel,' said Sionan. 'We will need a good old residual – there are few in the frozen north, and their knowledge is not great.'

'Oh! I expect that's why I'm here,' said the post, not looking its most erudite tied to a skateboard.

'That's good,' said Sionan.

'I have known Olga all of her life,' teddy piped up, 'and I was there when she took the grain.'

'This is all excellent!' Sionan said with a smile.

'But before we do anything, we must discuss practicalities,' said Yiptop.

'Practicalities?' said Sionan. 'We prepare the food and supplies we need, and sail tonight.'

'I can provide all the food and supplies we will need. My replication system will work within five thousand miles from the LIC.

'Wonderful, Yiptop. I will give you a full list of what we need. I'll be keeping a contingency stock, in case of any failure in your systems. You need to understand that approaching so close to the strong field of the magnetic north can have strange effects. Sometimes even my magic will not work as I would wish.'

'Tell us more about some of the hazards we may face on the journey, Sionan.'

'We will depart from these shores, relying on motor and sail. Our course will be north-westerly, passing south of the Faroes. Then we will encounter the icebergs of the north Atlantic, as we sail across the north Atlantic ridge, passing south of Iceland, into the Labrador basin, south of the King Frederik V1 coast. There we will pick up the relatively, and I stress relatively, warm tail end of the Gulf Stream. If the Air is on our side, this is where we will find out. With the amount of weaving we have to do there between pack ice and icebergs, we will need a kind wind to make reasonable time. This will take us north, into the Davis straits. There we will pass between Elsmere Island and Knud Ramussen Land. This is where we take to the land, and commence our trek across the frozen and virtually uninhabited path to the magnetic north. Any creatures we encounter other than the arctic fox will only desire to eat us.'

'Any abominable snowmen?' said Olga.

'I know of these, but they only live in the heights of the Himalayas. I've yet to hear of them in this northerly region. But I will tell you – abominable they are, but snowmen they are not. You will fair better against one of those than the merciless white bear of the polar north, and we will be lucky to pass through their domain without them knowing of us. This land trek will be the final part of our journey. It will be at the mercy of the Air, and will end, one way or another, at the whim of the Air.'

Yiptop had something to say.

'I have no doubt of your ability to captain this mission, and I don't doubt your extensive knowledge. But it does intrigue me to know how the Spirit of Leprechaun is related to this,even after benefiting from the stones explanation, as they see it.'

'That is to be sure a very good question. I will be happy to enlighten you,' Sionan responded. 'A long time ago, as early as 300 BC, Leprechauns were commonplace in Ireland. They were small peaceful people, no more than two feet tall and they had great power, unknown to most but still known to many.

'Many adventurous Irish sailors discovered a northern land, then known as Thule, situated one week's northerly sail from the north of Ireland. This land was much visited for its rich fishing and valued seal skins. Few but the peaceloving Leprechauns settled there. It was known to be a place of merciless cold. The Leprechauns were private people who were suited to quiet and philosophical lives, and they had many great powers which enabled them to survive comfortably in this frozen desert. The current few inhabitants are said to be descendants of the Irish sailors, interbred with the Viking people of Scandinavia, who also settled there. So you see both this land, as well as Ireland, can be considered the land of the Leprechaun. It is also the domain of the Air, and this is why I am called to this work, as Spirit of Leprechaun.'

'Cool!' said Yiptop. 'Nice to know we are in the best hands.'

'Good. Enough talk, we have work to do. I will get away and prepare for our departure. Meet me at the harbour at six o'clock and we will set sail. Is everyone happy?'

Murmurs of 'yes' surrounded Sionan.

'I'll bid you good day then, until later,' Sionan said with a smile as he left for the harbour.

CHAPTER TWELVE

Yiptop had been making some preparations of his own. He had spent the last few hours absorbed in his view-screen, and a large pile of equipment for the trip was beginning to mount up around him. And at his suggestion, Prudence was following Olga's training instructions. He anticipated that opportunities for Prudence to exercise would be limited on a long sea journey, so she may as well do some running around while she could.

'I think she's well-tired now,' said Olga. 'At least she'll be happy to rest for the first day or so.'

'That's probably the best we can do for her. It won't be much fun on that boat. It didn't look very big,' Yiptop replied, looking up from his screen.

'What's all this stuff, then?' Olga asked.

'The things on Sionan's list, plus a few bits and pieces to help us along.'

Olga looked through the pile. 'Snow shoes, fur coats. Gloves, hats, two sleds... What's this harness for?'

'That's for Prudence. I don't think she'll mind a bit of work, do you?'

'I suppose not. She's big and strong enough.'

'What's this?' Olga was looking at a strange electronic gadget, which looked like a calculator with four big removable plugs, each of which Yiptop had marked with their names: Olga, Prudence, Yiptop, and Sionan.

'That's the dire emergency lifesaver, which I hope we will never need. I figure if we fail and we're dying, we'll need an escape route.'

'And this electronic calculator will help?'

'It's not an electronic calculator. It's an emergency teleporter.'

'Will it sort of beam us home?'

'Not quite as easy as that. Teleporting is very new tech, even on Zog. It works and it's safe, but being converted to energy and back is about the most painful and uncomfortable experience in the universe. So it is only ever used to escape from a life-threatening situation. Even then, many who have used it have said they're not sure they wouldn't prefer to have died. You can be absolutely sure it's not fun.'

'How does it work?'

'It converts us, first to basic molecular structure, separating and digitising similar matter blocks.'

Olga interrupted. 'Please – not not the boy's version, Yiptop.'

'Okay, I have a DNA sample from each of us, from drink glasses. If we are really in trouble and about to die, I press this button and we get transported back to the LIC. One part of the DNA sample is in the LIC and one part on this plug. It's really the plug that is the vital part. Luckily The LIC comes with four in its standard emergency pack.'

'So we're not really risking our lives then? If we do fail, then instead of freezing to death in the Arctic, we teleport to the LIC, and come back to Earth and die anyway when the Air leaves!' said Olga, a little antagonistically.

'Give me some credit, Olga. If we fail, the Earth dies, do we have to die with it?

If we can escape at the last minute, at least we're alive.'

'What about everyone else?'

'Put it in perspective, Olga. Despite our final emergency measure, we are taking grave risks, and we are not by any means bound to have time to deploy it. We are taking these grave risks, and doing everything possible to save this world. If at the final moment our lives are saved, we are still serving continuance. It won't help anyone else if we needlessly die with them.'

'Okay, you're right as usual. Hate to sound like a ten-year-old, but are we nearly ready?' asked Olga, lightening up.

'We are ready,' Yiptop replied, 'and if we wander off to the harbour now, we will be just in time to meet Sionan.'

Yiptop and Olga set off with the post in tow on the skateboard, teddy under Olga's arm, and Prudence, walking smartly alongside.

'When we get on the boat I will port all the supplies on to it. The LIC will go into auto orbit and stay above us till we need it,' said Yiptop.

Arriving at the harbour, it was a clear day out to sea. They could see Sionan leaving the boat in the tender. Yiptop said dubiously,

'The boat hasn't got any bigger! I don't know how we're all going to fit on that for the next week or so.'

'We'll be fine,' said Olga. 'We don't need much space. I'm sure it will be well organised.'

They headed down to the jetty and met Sionan there as he arrived.

'Sure I like to see punctuality! It's good to see you all. Yiptop, do you have all the supplies on my list?'

'Yes, all ready to teleport to the boat,' said Yiptop.

'Sure I'll never get used to these space gadgets! Give me good old Leprechaun magic anytime,' Sionan said, smiling his ever-present – and magic in itself – smile. He picked Olga up and gave her a huge hug. 'Are you ready for the adventure of a lifetime, Angel?'

'Yes, we're all ready, Sionan,' Olga replied warmly.

'We'll all be squeezing into this tender, and making our way to my boat. I have it all ready for you. You'll love my boat – it's been my home for a long time.'

They all got into Sionan's tender, and Yiptop's first shock arrived. Sionan picked up the oars and held them in place, but he did not row. He did not row, but still the tender started to move smoothly towards the boat.

'You're not rowing!' said Yiptop.

'Do you know, Yiptop, it's a funny old world, and with what you just said, you've assured me that it's a funny old world where you come from too.'

'How's that? I only said you're not rowing.'

'And if I was cleaning my shoes, sure enough someone would walk by and say "cleaning your shoes then, Sionan, are you?" I think what you meant to ask was "how is it, Sionan, that the little boat is moving and you're not rowing?"'

'Okay – how?'

'Because the little boat knows I want it to move.'

'How can the boat know you want it to move?'

'Sure if I didn't want it to move, then why, tell me, would I have picked up the oars? Now a small tender may not be the cleverest thing in the world, but it knows very well that if a man picks up the oars, he'll be wanting to go somewhere. What's more, having just left the boat and collected some people it wouldn't take the little tender a wild guess to know that I wanted to go back to the boat.'

'Yes, but how do you know it knows?'

'Sure I'll be worrying about you in a minute, Yiptop. If the little tender didn't know I wanted to move, they why would it be moving?'

'What I mean, Sionan, is – by what communicative process does it know, and by what automotive power is it moving?'

'Magic, of course. Leprechaun magic.'

'There's no such thing as magic.

'Then there's no such thing as spacemen.'

'How am I here, then?'

'Sure because you are talking to me, and you tell me you're from Zog, and I have to say, you produced a fine breakfast from nothing at all.'

'So you accept that spacemen exist!' Yiptop was getting excited, thinking he was getting somewhere.

'Sure okay, and is the boat moving?'

'Yes.'

'Am I rowing?'

'No.'

'Then you'll have to accept that magic exists.'

'I will for now,' said Yiptop, smiling and frustrated at the same time.

'Yiptop, that's the first time I've seen you confused,' said Olga, giggling in delight.

They arrived at Sionan's boat. It was, to say the least, an unlikely craft in which to undertake such a voyage. It looked about ten feet long, quite narrow, and surprisingly for such a small boat, ketch rigged. It looked like a magnificent and beautiful sailing yacht, but in miniature.

'Well here we are. Now, you all keep still and leave everything to me while I get us on board,' said Sionan.

Yiptop endured still further confusion as he watched this process. The tender rested about two feet from the boat. A wooden boom swung out from the boat and a rope descended from it. On the end of the rope was a hook, which Sionan attached to a set of ropes on the tender. Sionan smiled, and the tender started to rise towards the boom. As it reached the top, the boom swung around and lowered the tender onto the deck. At this point, both Olga and Yiptop were rubbing their eyes in complete confusion. It seemed very clear that the boat they had landed on was not the boat they had seen from the water. This boat was at least four times the size.

'Welcome aboard *Ice Dancer*!' said Sionan.

'The boat's called *Ice Dancer*?' asked Olga.

'Sure, she is called *Ice Dancer*, and ice dancing is what she does best, as you will soon enough see,' Sionan replied, proudly.

'She's magnificent,' said Olga, struck by the beauty of the boat.

'She's big,' said Yiptop, struck by his inability to verbalise his current thoughts as he stood in full fly-catching mode, mouth open in disbelief.

'You have something to say, Yiptop?' asked Sionan.

'Sionan, this boat is at least four times the size of the boat we saw from the water.'

'No, Yiptop. *Ice Dancer* is the size she has always been.'

'Sorry, Sionan it looked about a quarter of this size, from down in the water,' said Yiptop, rubbing his eyes and almost ready to believe that his eyes were deceiving him.

'Sure I'll not play games with you, what you're seeing here is Leprechaun magic again.'

'So you made the boat bigger? What's the point? Why not just keep it big in the first place? There's plenty of room in the sea.'

'As I told you, she is the same size as always. I've not made her any bigger. *Ice Dancer* is a small boat, no more than ten feet long. Her small size is a great advantage negotiating small passages between pack ice.'

'But Sionan, I can see that the boat we are standing on is at least forty feet long,' said Yiptop, very keen not to offend, but equally keen to insist that the boat was bigger.

'I'll put you out of your confusion. You see, the Leprechauns are very good at making things small. Try this old pirate game of walking the plank and you'll not doubt that I'm right.'

Sionan secured a plank, extending off the side of the boat.

'Now Yiptop, step on to the plank and walk a little way from us. Careful not to fall off.'

Olga was watching with amazement. As Yiptop walked along the plank, he became a giant of four times his normal size.

'Yiptop, you're huge!' Olga shouted to him.

'You're all tiny! This is amazing!' shouted Yiptop from the plank.

'Come on back in now! Enough fun and games – we need to set sail. Sure I can never resist that little demonstration! It's such a pleasure to see people's reaction,' said Sionan, pleased with himself at breaking the ice with his new guests on *Ice Dancer*. Yiptop stepped back onto *Ice Dancer* and as he stepped down, he instantly regained his proportional size.

'Are you okay, Yiptop?' Olga asked, as he looked a bit freaked out.

'I'm not used to magic. It hasn't existed on my world for a long time. There have been legends of its existence, but no-one really believed them. I'm fine, though, don't worry. But I suspect somehow that we have more to come.'

They set sail; a surprisingly uncomplicated procedure, it seemed. Sionan sat at the wheel, which he called the helm. He had a fairly tall seat, which gave him a commanding view. Olga and Yiptop sat around him on lower seats. Yiptop had ported the supplies and all had been put away in the area Sionan called 'below'. This consisted of a large room with a table and benches, a small but adequate galley at one end, and bunk beds at the other. Near the helm were things called capstans and cleats. They seemed to deal with all the ropes, which Sionan called sheets. This surprised Olga, as she really thought the sails would be called sheets. The sheets and capstans all seemed to have minds of their own as did the cleats. They would tighten and loosen at regular intervals, seeming to follow some sort of unspoken commands from Sionan. There was a big thing which Sionan called the boom, which would occasionally fly from one side to the other and cause the boat to lean in the opposite direction. The only person who had to duck to avoid decapitation by this boom was Sionan. He would however shout, very loudly in his deep voice, just before the boom went across. Olga assumed this was some kind of warning for everyone. He shouted something that sounded like 'reiy bout'. Olga would later realise that he was actually saying 'ready about', and that this whole procedure was called 'going about'. At the back of the boat was another small sail, like a smaller version of the main sail. Olga got the impression that this one just did its own thing. On closer observation and further consultation with Yiptop, Olga realised that all of these things were being instructed by certain facial expressions produced by Sionan.

Olga and Yiptop had spent a good half hour in hilarious amusement, trying to look at bits of rope and construct tighten and loosen expressions on their faces, all to great comedic effect, but to no practical avail, as nothing took any notice of them at all.

Sionan had spent a fair bit of time generously explaining the basics of sailing to Yiptop. He had absorbed it all just like a boy with a new gadget. He had understood well, and Sionan was very impressed – he was making a friend of Yiptop. Yiptop had even understood how that little sail at the back of the boat would help them to manoeuvre in pack ice.

They were all very tired and had slept very well the first night. The accommodation could only be described as grand and very comfortable.

The next morning they were all out on deck. Yiptop had dragged the post out as well, and Olga had brought teddy. They figured that being residuals, it was their job to absorb information and remember it, and they would get more information on deck than below.

'It's a big boat,' said the post.

'No, you are a smaller post. But don't worry – when we get off, you'll be bigger again,' Olga replied, comfortingly.

'Oh! That will be Leprechaun magic,' said the post.

'While you're here, post, would you help me with something? I'm a little confused?'

'I'll do what I can,' it replied, caringly.

'It's just that I've been thinking about the proper order of things, and how the Gods, trees, residuals and people fit in to it all. It seems to me that most things seem to be cleverer than people, yet people seem to have a position of greater importance. I do realise of course that I may be seeing the important place of people from the point of view of being one.'

'Oh, but you are quite right in one way. People do have the favour of the gods. They are the children of the gods, it is even said, made in the image of the gods, although that may be stretching it a bit. But in another way you're a bit adrift. I'll explain. You see my dear, you must not confuse knowledgeable with clever, nor infinite memory with clever. Clever is something else altogether.'

'How do you mean?' Olga asked.

'Well you see, residuals and trees really only store information. We residuals process it to a certain extent and make sense of it. The trees process and refine information to an incredible degree with their endless thinking. But you see, all of this processing never includes creative or original thought. It's called vertical thinking, and that's all that we and the trees are capable of.'

'Vertical thinking? Sounds like you can't think lying down!' Olga chuckled.

'Vertical thinking is the process of placing one thought upon another then another in layers. The basis of the thought has to come from an external input, like for example, seeing something a person has done. This then starts a process of interdependent thinking, each thought giving rise to the next thought and the next and so on, building in vertical layers. People however are quite different in their thinking ability, and much cleverer. A person is the only sentient on the planet, who can create original thought, invent new thought, thought which is independent in its own right. A person can pick out of nothingness a completely new notion. That's cleverness, and only people are gifted with this.'

'What about magic, like Sionan can do?'

'Only very special selected people can do magic.'

'Magic is a direct gift from the Gods and is only entrusted to people who are doing the work of the gods. Like Sionan and Prudence, and you.'

'Me? But I can't do magic!'

'Oh, but you will, my dear. You are the Angel of the Moo… him. You will do magic. You are young yet, and will need to learn about your magic skills. Prudence will also have some magic powers which will become apparent when they are needed.'

While this was going on, Yiptop had wandered off to sit with Sionan, who was as usual dutifully occupied at the helm.

'So when are you going to tell me how all this magic stuff works then Sionan?' Yiptop asked.

'Yiptop, to be sure, your people are very advanced. I can see that by your advanced gadgetry and from talking to you. You have a very advanced and informed attitude to peace and purpose, and how you fit in the proper order of things. I must admit to some ambivalence where gadgets are concerned, but I always had my magic to get me by and so never had the need for gadgets. I'm impressed by your sense of honour and duty, and by your courage and willingness to put yourself at risk for a greater purpose. Add to that your people's understanding of greed, pride, and other evils, and we have a very great and advanced people. But despite all this, you still suffer from the need to know, and from the delusion that you can know. Even, if I might add, from the delusion that it is desirable to know things that are not for our knowing.'

'We all like to know things, Sionan,' Yiptop replied defensively.

'Sure it's good to know, if there's purpose in knowing, but needing to know for the sake of knowing – well, that's another thing altogether. Knowledge is like a Russian doll. Well almost, anyway.'

'What's a Russian doll?' Yiptop asked.

'A wooden doll that you can break in half, to discover another smaller doll inside, then you break that one and find yet another smaller doll inside that. This goes on and on, and you keep getting smaller and smaller dolls. Then in the end, you get to a very small doll, just like the one you started with, but much smaller. And this one doesn't open. It's solid.'

'How is that like knowledge?'

'Well you ask a question and get an answer, that gives rise to another question and another answer, then in the end, theoretically you get to the gods, because they are at the root of creation. You won't go further, and they will only tell you what they wish to, and you'll be surprised to find out that they already have. Is it not better, Yiptop, at some point to accept that there are things we are not supposed to know.'

'Like how magic works?'

'Exactly. Truth is, I don't know myself. It's a gift of the Gods in order to do their work, and I don't question the gods.'

'So you think it's not good to question.'

'No! I think it's great to question, but it's not so good always to expect an answer. The question opens a door, the need for an answer seeks to close it, and I think doors are better left open, especially doors in the mind.'

'You're a wise man, Sionan. I'll give that some serious thought.'

'While you're thinking there, Yiptop, could you get to work with your wonderful gadgets and produce me another glass of Guinness like you did before? I've a terrible thirst sure I have.'

Yiptop got to work and in seconds a very large four-pint glass of Guinness appeared in front of Sionan. They both roared with laughter.

'If I drink that we'll be a long time getting anywhere, while I'm sailing us round in circles!' said Sionan, through the laughter.

Yiptop went below to fetch a normal size glass and they decanted a normal-sized potion in to it.

'While we were talking, did you not notice something, Yiptop?' Sionan asked. 'Sure when you're sailing you have to stop and smell the flowers. In other words, you have to notice what's going on around you. Do you not see the sails?'

Yiptop looked and saw how slack the sails had gone.

'What does that tell us?' Yiptop asked.

'Together with those clouds up there, it tells us we've an almighty storm brewing.'

They looked ahead at a black heavy sky in the distance.

'Aye, and it's heading this way. That's a storm to make the bravest sailor shiver in his boots, especially in a ten-foot boat.'

'A bad one, then?' said Yiptop, unaccustomed to being at the mercy of the elements.

'We are about to see the other side of the coin,' Sionan said ominously.

'How do you mean?'

'Small boats are great in ice, not so good in big storms.'

'Can you magic it bigger?'

'Leprechaun magic specialises in small, not big. But if it really gets tough I can get some help,' Sionan said reassuringly.

Sionan left the helm in calmness for a few minutes and went to stand at the bow of the boat. He let out a sharp whistle, just like the one that called Prudence when they first met. He then returned to the helm.

'If it gets rough, which I expect it will, I may ask you and Olga to go below, for safety. Meanwhile would you go below and make sure everything is closed up and secure? We're in for a rough ride.'

Yiptop went below and told Olga and they went about the job of securing everything and closing all the hatches. They left Prudence down below and sat at the helm with Sionan.

Suddenly, out of nowhere, two massive black creatures the size of large oil tankers rose out of the water either side of *Ice Dancer*. The disturbance rocked the boat violently. Olga and Yiptop held onto their seats.

'Whales!' said Olga, in panic. 'Huge whales!'

Of course, the whales appeared to be four times bigger than they actually were.

'What are we going to do, Sionan? They could easily sink us if they wanted to, and with the storm coming as well,' said Yiptop, also panicking a bit.

'Well I'm sure they'll not be sinking the boat, especially as they're here to help. I just called them a few minutes ago,' said Sionan, as cool as a cucumber.

The two whales re-submerged and stayed very close either side of *Ice Dancer*, just below the surface.

The air was still. The sea was as calm as a solid sheet of ice. The occasional ray of sunshine leaked through a gap in the heavy black sky, only to be reflected straight back by the sheer surface of the sea. There was an eerie silence. Blackness upon blackness took over and turned day into night. Every few minutes there came a slight and short gust of wind, there and then gone. Olga felt a single drop of rain on her hand, just one – then seconds later another.

'Go below, my Angel,' said Sionan, not taking his eyes off the sea as he said it.

Olga went below.

'Yiptop – clip this to your belt!' Sionan handed a fixed short line to Yiptop.

The sea like a sheet of flexible glass bent downwards, taking *Ice Dancer* down with it. In every direction, all that could be seen was a solid wall of sea completely surrounding them. As it bottomed out it started to rise rapidly, till all horizons disappeared. They were perched on a mountain peak of sea, teetering and pitching as *Ice Dancer* struggled to gain purchase on the evasive surface. Yiptop left his seat as *Ice Dancer* dropped back down in a failed attempt to descend with the same violent speed as the sea descended. As it reached the bottom again, Yiptop reconnected with his seat with a hard thud. It was like the sea was flexing its muscles and bending down then up again, first slowly but gradually becoming more rhythmic and violent, then less regular, changing rhythm like a vicious war dance. Then the wind came, whipping around *Ice Dancer*'s mast like a raging bull, stabbing at the small boat, teasing it, pressing it down against the sea, then releasing it and spinning it from side to side in a vicious game of cat and mouse, launching great sheets of rain with each gust. Suddenly night became day, but just for one second, as the flash of lightening played out its short life, to give birth to another seconds later.

Still Sionan sat solidly at the helm as if commanding *Ice Dancer* to stay upright and not spill her contents into the sea.

'We'll not get through this without some help!' shouted Sionan.

Sionan let out two sharp whistles, just before another ear-splitting boom of thunder over took the soundscape. 'There's more to come, by the sound of it!' Sionan shouted, to no-one in particular. Yiptop had never before in his life witnessed at first hand the violence of the elements! He was very scared, and at the same time in awe of the great power at play, and his insignificance in it. The pitch and toss was becoming more violent and capsize seemed imminent. *Ice Dancer* had fought bravely with the great captain at the helm, but she wasn't built for this. With her short bulb keel, she did not possess the inherent stability to cope.

The two gigantic whales rose from the surface during a split second of respite, when the seascape had momentarily looked somewhere near normal. They rose in unison like two formation swimmers in an old movie. At either side of *Ice Dancer* they pressed against the small hull, their soft flexible bodies giving way to contain her between them. Gripped firmly between the two whales *Ice Dancer* was carried away at alarming speed by the two whales working as a team to extricate the boat from danger. This rapid rollercoaster ride went on for twenty minutes or so, as the sky continued to play out its battle of power with the sea. At the end of the ride they were in what seemed like another world, much like the one that had been replaced by the violent storm they had just left. The whales moved apart, releasing *Ice Dancer* to the water and moving away from her sides.

Sionan stood his full height and whistled loudly to the whales. In reply they leapt from the water like two hugely oversized dolphins, then dived and went on their way, back to whatever their lives held for them, to whatever they did when they weren't saving very small boats in very big storms for their friend the Spirit of Leprechaun.

'Sure there are times when you need a friend,' said Sionan looking weary. 'Go below and check everything is okay, Yiptop.'

Yiptop unclipped his belt and went below.

'You okay, Olga?' said Yiptop, his voice shaky from the experience.

'Yeah, I'm fine. that was scary! We were flying at one point, I'm sure.'

'We were carried out of the storm between the two whales. That was the most amazing thing I have ever seen in my life! But it's all clear now, Olga. You can come back on deck.'

The next few days went smoothly, making good time in perfect wind. The days were getting longer and longer, the nights eventually disappearing altogether. They had reached the place where a day endured half the year, to be followed in turn by the long winter's night. It was getting colder, and the Air was getting cleaner and fresher. Olga felt there was something incredibly pure and natural about this place. She was not at all surprised the Air had made its home near here. There was a divine unspoilt beauty, an undiluted richness.

It was on day six that they encountered their first iceberg – a pure white floating island, big enough for a small town. Olga didn't know any more if things were really as big as they seemed, or if it was an illusion born of their downsizing. It didn't matter, though – by any measure, this iceberg was big, majestic and beautiful. Reaching out of the water like a frosted mountain peak, yet moving, floating rising up and down again, at the whim of the mighty sea.

CHAPTER THIRTEEN

'Wow! Look, Yiptop. That must be Iceland!' said Olga.

'Looks a bit small for a whole country, and I think we're way past Iceland. Maybe it's a small island,' Yiptop replied.

'Sionan, have we got time to stop at that island? It's only a couple of miles away,' asked Olga.

Sionan was concentrating at the helm with his usual diligence. 'Island! Now that's the best I've heard. What you're looking at there is a treacherous beast, if ever there was one!'

'A treacherous beast?' said Olga, not really understanding.

'Sure what you see there is an iceberg,' said Sionan, in a woefully respectful tone.

'An iceberg! Like the one that sank the Titanic?'

'Sure, and a more treacherous and dangerous devil you'll not see in your life, my Angel.' Sionan looked very serious.

'It looks so beautiful and peaceful,' said Olga.

'If every treacherous beast we encountered wore a sign saying "look out for me", what an easy and safe life we'd have, sure we would.'

'What's the danger, Sionan? It's at least a mile away and doesn't look as if it's about to attack us,' asked Yiptop in a way that suggested that he already knew the answer, a quite charming trait of Yiptop's that sometimes irritated Sionan.

'Listen up now, and I'll tell you a few things about icebergs. This all relates to one of the great men of all time, a great mathematician by the name of Leonardo Fibonacci. He was to open doors to understanding the world we live in, such that nothing would ever be the same after him – at least that is for those who truly understood him, but we'll talk more of him, and others like him. An iceberg sits in the water showing you only roughly one third of its great mass, the other two thirds hidden beneath the water. Now a fool would think that something of such apparent beauty would be courteous enough to observe the symmetry of carrying the same shape under the water as above. Not so, and there are even those who believe that these frozen sirens use their beauty to tempt the natural comfort in symmetry to that conclusion. In this lies one treachery of this beast, we don't know anything about the form of this iceberg below the water. Its razor sharp weaponry is waiting to cut to shreds the underside of an unsuspecting boat passing by to admire its beauty. If that were the only threat, then we would simply stay a safe enough distance. There is another more deadly and unpredictable danger from these devils. They float in the water towards warmer climes, and in doing so they gradually melt in the sun's rays, reducing in size as they go. But as this is happening they are eroded from beneath by currents of water. As a result, suddenly in a split second, far beneath the surface, a large piece may break away, upsetting the balance of the floating island. The whole thing, the size of a town, then flips in the water and rolls itself over, creating a wave that would capsize and swallow up a boat ten times the size of *Ice Dancer*, all in a dreadful instant. So you see I'd be happier if we were so far away, we couldn't even see it. I've heard it said that one iceberg can spoil your whole day!' Sionan lightened up with a broad smile.

'Will there be more?' asked Yiptop.

'As we are shortly entering the Labrador Sea we will encounter many, large and small, and we may have to pass so close you could almost touch them.'

'That's a bit dodgy,' said Olga.

'Don't you worry, my Angel, with the magic of the Leprechaun, we'll not be falling victim to any iceberg – *Ice Dancer* will get us through.'

They sailed on through the cold Labrador Sea, *Ice Dancer*'s lithe form slipping between more icebergs. Olga's sleeping habits were adapting to a new regime, a regime that better suited the endless days and absence of night. The new order was four hours asleep and four hours awake. Sionan, who was blessed with seemingly limitless stamina, needed no more than an hour of sleep every eight. Yiptop, of course, only rested, but his rest periods tied in with Olga's sleep hours. The wind till now was kind, and they were ahead of Sionan's time estimates and rapidly approaching what Sionan called the Ice Maze.

The three were sitting in their usual positions either side of the helm.

'So tell us more about this Fibonancy, Sionan,' said Olga with a charm that despite her ten years was becoming what could only be described as erudite.

'Sure you mean Fibonacci, my Angel.'

'Yes – what's he got to do with icebergs?'

'I've thought about telling you all about the often misunderstood conundrum of knowledge, understanding and wisdom, and the way in which people like Fibonacci and Lao Tzu transcended the norm and dealt with that conundrum in a way that seemed to evade others. But I think, my Angel, that this is neither the time nor the place, and if you'll be patient, until after our audience with the Air, we may find we have more time for such things.'

They sailed on into the Labrador Sea, an ever-changing vista of sheer frozen whiteness, to Olga's eyes a veritable winter wonderland of water in its various forms. From the vapour of the clouds and eerie mists, to the lightness of snow and the solid steel coldness of ice, a reality of nature untouched by human hand lay before her. No great artist with all his craft and insight could ever justify what stark beauty lay in every direction before her, behind her and above and below.

'Do you know, Olga, we're sitting on top of the world. When you've seen this sight once, sure nothing will ever look quite the same to you again. You are seeing the greatness of water, a greatness it achieves by doing nothing more than being water – no tricks, no knowledge, merely the simplicity of being what it is is great enough in itself. No more is needed of it,' said Sionan.

'Are people like that?'

'They sure enough could be, and they'd need not much more than to stop trying, and just be. You'd be sure sometimes that the most basic verb in any language – to be – was the most difficult to understand.'

Time went by and the combination of kind winds and Sionan's magic transformed a potentially death-defying voyage into a walk in the park. There were some things that Sionan had said that had started Olga thinking, exploring her mind. In so doing, she was continuing to discover new avenues of her mind, new ways of reasoning hitherto undiscovered.

'Look ahead. You'll see that we are now arriving at the Ice Maze. This is where we pass, or don't pass, at the mercy of the Air. If the Air truly believes in what we are about, and you can be sure that the Air is aware of every word and deed since we left Whitehaven, then we will get through,' said Sionan.

'Do you mean to say that we can't get through this without the will of the Air?' asked Yiptop.

'The way I would normally approach the Ice Maze is to feel my way through and let the magic of the Leprechauns guide me to the right course. That magic is at the mercy of the Air, as every breath we take and everything we do is at the mercy of the Air.'

'Isn't it just a matter of finding pathways wide enough for *Ice Dancer* to pass?' Yiptop asked.

'True, but you could take a pathway, and find that after a hundred miles it could be blocked. Then you would have to return and choose another path. It's possible to spend your life and not find a way through. That's why it's the Ice Maze.'

'So what will be your approach now?' asked Olga.

'I think we will heave to right here and wait. We'll see what happens.'

'Heave to what, Sionan?' Olga asked, puzzled.

'Sorry! Heave to means *to park*.'

'So we are just going to sit here and wait,' said Yiptop.

'Sure I have a feeling that's what we should be doing right now,' Sionan affirmed.

'But what are we waiting for?' Yiptop asked.

'First of all, if you look upwards…'

Yiptop looked up and a strange blackness seemed to cover the sky, but only in a large circle above them. Beyond that circle, the sky seemed clear.

'What's that, Sionan? And why has the wind dropped to nothing?'

'To be truthful, Yiptop. I haven't seen anything like that before now, and it doesn't represent any weather system in my experience.'

Olga came up from below, where she had been sitting with Prudence and reminiscing with teddy.

'Wow, Sionan! What's the sky doing, and where's the wind gone?'

'We were just noticing, Olga.'

'What are we going to do? Could we use the engine, if there's no wind?'

'We'll not want to be using the engines through the Ice Maze, my Angel. We'll be needing the wind for that.'

'The wind and the Air are the same thing, so maybe we should just wait and see what happens,' said Olga.

Yiptop and Sionan roared with laughter.

'What's funny about that?' Olga asked.

'That's exactly what Sionan said! I think I've got two magicians ganging up on me!' said Yiptop smiling.

They all sat and had a bite to eat and drink. Then Yiptop and Olga went below to get some clothing together for the coldness they were expecting to endure from here on. It was cold already, but Sionan had told them that it could get much worse.

'Of course,' said Yiptop, 'none of these clothes or shoes are going to go anywhere near fitting us till we get off the boat.'

'True, they're all four times too big, so we'll have to wait, but Sionan must be keeping the deck areas warm somehow. I haven't felt as cold as I should.'

'Let's go on deck and see what's happening.'

They took up their places near the helm with Sionan.

'Look,' said Sionan. 'There's a small hole in the black cloud above us.'

'Yes, and something strange is going on. Look at my hair!' said Olga.

Olga's hair was literally standing upright, pointing alarmingly skyward.

'This is the first time in all my years at sea that I have experienced a wind going straight up!' said Sionan.

Ice Dancer began to turn on its own axis, slowly at first, then becoming more of a spin.

'Get below, both of you!' Sionan ordered.

'What about you, Sionan?' said Yiptop as he got up to obey the serious order.

'Do you think I'm crazy? I'm coming too!'

Sionan followed them below and closed everything.

'We'll sit tight and see what it's all about. It could only be the Air behind this.'

Ice Dancer was turning, spinning around and around, getting faster. All three of them were pinned to their seats. Prudence jumped up onto the seat next to Sionan and was equally held in place by the spinning motion. As the spinning got faster, Olga became dizzy and could barely see. Yiptop and Sionan seemed less affected.

The spinning motion stopped accelerating and began to level off. They were all suddenly aware of an upward movement as *Ice Dancer* lifted out of the water, and in a screwing motion began to rise skywards.

Sionan managed to turn his head and look through the porthole.

'Sure this is the strangest thing I ever did see! We must be two hundred feet from the sea, and still going up!'

'Some weird things are happening on this planet!' Yiptop remarked.

'I just wish my head was not spinning the opposite way to the boat… and my tummy doesn't feel too good,' said Olga, who had clearly felt better.

As *Ice Dancer* rose relentlessly upwards, it became lighter and warmer as they approached the hole in the cloud.

'Do you notice it's getting warmer?' said Sionan.

'Yes it is,' Yiptop replied.

'Sure this is very strange!'

The spinning began to slow and *Ice Dancer* passed through the hole in the cloud. The hole closed beneath them, and the spinning slowed to a stop. All was quiet and peaceful. Olga lay down.

'We've stopped spinning, and we've stopped rising,' Sionan said.

'*You* may have, but I'm still spinning!' said Olga.

Sionan took another look through the porthole, this time getting up to get a better view. 'We're through the hole. You two wait here. I'm going on deck to take a look,' he said..

'Are you sure that's a good idea?' said Yiptop.

'Frankly, no, but I'm going anyway!' Sionan replied making light of his courage.

'How are you feeling, Olga?' Yiptop enquired.

'I'm slowing down a bit. I think I need a drink,' Olga replied.

'Orange juice?' said Yiptop.

'No, I think I'd better have water,' said Olga, still sounding a bit queasy.

Yiptop handed Olga a glass of water and she sat up to drink it.

'Better now?' Yiptop asked.

'Yes, I think I'm okay now.'

'You can both come out now and take a look what's happening,' Sionan shouted.

Yiptop and a slightly wobbly Olga ventured warily out on deck.

Ice Dancer was on a cloud. The sun was shining and by the look of the sails, she was sailing along happily as if at sea.

'We seem to be sailing on the clouds, Sionan!' said Yiptop.

'We sure are, and we're going in the right direction too,' said Sionan.

'I've been meaning to ask you, you don't use any charts or navigation instruments, yet even here on the clouds, you seem to know our exact position and direction. How is that?' Yiptop asked.

'Sure you pick a strange time to ask. Have you heard of a homing pigeon?'

'Yes. They use them for racing and passing messages.'

'They always know where they are and where they're going. They never use charts nor look at the sun and stars. It is said that they use a simple system of triangulation with the north and south magnetic poles. It is said that seagoing Leprechauns use the same system. Like me, they always know exactly where they are and where they're going. And we're headed north at a greater speed than it appears.'

True enough, *Ice Dancer* was sailing along, its sheets, cleats and sails doing much the same as they had been on their long sea voyage so far. The only difference seemed to be that they were sailing the clouds and not the sea.

'I think we can safely assume that this is the work of the Air. We should just relax and see what happens,' said Sionan.

'I've given up safely assuming anything, but I don't see what we can do but wait,' Olga said.

They waited, sailing rather majestically, Sionan thought, across the skies of the frozen north. They were comfortable and adjusted to this new reality, but they were all wondering what was coming next.

CHAPTER FOURTEEN

'So, how are we going to get down from here,
Sionan?' Yiptop asked.

'Sure it's no problem at all! You see when we arrive at
our destination, near the Lincoln Sea, I'll just call up
my old friend Jack on my mobile phone. Jack will
have his giant beanstalk ready, and we'll climb right
down,' Sionan replied.

'Jack! Who's he?' said Yiptop, astonished.

'He's pulling your leg,' said Olga.

'Sionan, it was a serious question!' Yiptop remarked
indignantly.

'Yiptop, we're sailing along on the clouds, way up in
the sky, and you think how are we going to get down
is a serious question. I think, as we don't know how
we got up here, and we sure enough don't know how

we're staying up here, then to ask how we get down might just be a little bit academic.'

'So what do we do?' asked Yiptop, never very happy with unscientific stratagems which result in inaction.

'What we do is accept that whatever got us up here knows more about levitation than we do, and hope that it provides us with an eventual safe landing.'

'I suppose there's not much else we can do,' said Yiptop, resigned.

'Sure, but if you do get a better idea, please share it with us, Yiptop.'

Ice Dancer sailed on over the smoothly undulating clouds, with no interruptions other than the odd visit from some very confused birds. Our intrepid voyagers had all but lost their sense of time.

'Sionan, how many days have we been sailing?' Olga asked.

'Sure my reckoning tells me it's ten days,' Sionan replied.

'I'm sure it's eleven days,' Yiptop interrupted.

'There's only one way to be sure,' Sionan decided.

'We'll ask a residual. They have a perfect sense of time.'

Olga went below to fetch teddy.

'Teddy, how long have we been sailing?' Olga asked.

'We've been on this boat for eleven and a half days. If there was a night, we'd be in the middle of it, on day eleven,' teddy responded, delighted at last, to contribute something useful.

'Well done, Yiptop! You got the closest guess. Sure there are no flies on you!' Sionan commented magnanimously.

'Thank you, Sionan. It was just a guess though,' said Yiptop.

'Sure my timing may be adrift, but I can assure you there's nothing wrong with my positioning. We're very near to the northernmost part of Knud Ramussen Land. I don't know if the Air means to take us all the way, or put us down to complete our journey on foot,' Sionan announced.

'Why would he bring us this far and then leave us to continue on foot?' asked Yiptop.

'Sure the Air is not renowned for being gratuitously helpful. You have to remember that interference is generally frowned upon. It will be believing that we should be running our own lives as far as possible.'

'But it's interfered by more or less deciding to leave the planet and put an end to everything. I would call that fairly serious intervention!' Yiptop said.

'That's different. It's part of a much wider-reaching universe issue, and not the Air's decision as such. You know that in the proper order of things, a planet cannot be allowed to put universal continuance at risk. The Air would never want to leave this planet if it had any choice, and this intervention of the Air and Moon is an attempt to gain that choice, by satisfying the Gods that the risk is under control. If you ask me, this whole thing smells of direct intervention from the Gods themselves, may they not strike me down for saying so.'

'I have to say I have the same view, including the not-strike-me-down bit,' Yiptop admitted.

'Sure enough, and you'll not be wrong.'

The ship began to slow down.

'Ah, we're slowing down,' said Sionan. 'I don't think it'll be too long before we know what happens next.'

Sionan's face showed his ominous look, which usually preceded a discomforting event.

'Whatever the Air decides to do next, I just hope it can manage it without all that spinning. That made me quite ill,' said Olga.

Sionan looked over the side of *Ice Dancer*. 'The cloud is clearing beneath us. I can almost see to the ground.'

The cloud beneath *Ice Dancer* was becoming thinner by the minute. She was beginning to rock gently from side to side. This rocking motion became wider and started to pendulum from one direction to another, rising at the end of each sweep and descending in the middle. They were gradually losing altitude, rather like a leaf falling from a tree on a still autumn day. *Ice Dancer* bounced gently from one arc to the next, slowly sinking down and down until, splash, they were back in the icy water.

'Cool!' said Olga. 'Much better than all that spinning.'

'Definitely better than spinning. Where are we, Sionan?' said Yiptop.

'We are just where I thought, slightly north of Knud Ramussen Land to the west of the Eurasia Basin, more perfectly placed than even I could have managed myself. There is no more sailing from here on, not without some very sudden global warming,' said Sionan, proudly.

'Are you sure this isn't all Leprechaun magic, and not the work of the Air at all, Sionan?' Olga said, accusingly.

'Now if I had the magic to sail the clouds like that, do you think for one second that I'd be bothering to sail the sea?' Sionan replied dismissively, his radiant smile warming the cold air around them.

'I'm just a bit suspicious by nature,' said Olga, almost apologetically.

'My Angel, such suspicion may well keep you alive one day, and I'm flattered that you would think my humble magic could be so powerful. You can rest assured, though, that such magic is beyond the Leprechauns, and I had nothing to do with our voyage across the sky.'

'So, now what?' said Yiptop.

'So now we have some unloading to do,' Sionan replied.

The air had placed *Ice Dancer* conveniently against a bank of ice which was just above the water line.

'We'll load all the supplies into the smaller tender and hoist it ashore, then we'll get ourselves into the larger tender and hoist ourselves ashore,' Sionan commanded.

They all worked hard loading the tender and getting everything ashore. Once they had landed themselves ashore with all the supplies, *Ice Dancer* dutifully loaded the tenders back on board.

'It's good to see no-one is complaining of the cold. Ordinarily we'd all be dying or dead by now. I have my magic to keep me warm. Olga, you must have the

same,' Sionan said smiling knowingly at Olga.

'I'm fine. I can sense that it's colder than I've ever

experienced, but I feel okay,' Olga replied.

'We Zoggers are okay for a very wide range of

temperatures. This is well within the lower limits,'

Yiptop said.

'Prudence looks quite happy as well, and she's

certainly happy to be back on land,' Olga added.

Prudence was at present running around like some

deranged lunatic, in ever-decreasing circles, it seemed, simply

exercising the fact that she now could. They loaded the sleds

and harnessed the one carrying the post to the now calmer

Prudence, who looked perfectly at home with it. Sionan

insisted on pulling the other one; compared to his huge bulk,

it didn't look at all inappropriate. They looked possibly the

oddest band of arctic explorers ever to set foot in this frozen

waste.

'My instructions are to head north until the Air makes contact with us,' said Sionan.

The weather was clear, and it was crisp underfoot from recent snow as they trekked northwards for a full tiring eight hours. At the end of this eight-hour trek, they decided to set up camp so they could eat and rest.

Yiptop and Sionan set about unpacking and erecting the tent, while Olga removed Prudence's harness and put down a waterproof sheet for her to lie on.

'I'll get us all some food,' said Yiptop, as they finished with the tent.

He materialised his view-screen and proceeded to take the orders. Unlike previous occasions, the food was not quickly forthcoming. In fact, despite Yiptop's many attempts, it didn't arrive at all.

'This is both very strange and very worrying. I seem to have lost contact with the LIC,' Yiptop said, frustrated.

'Sure I did tell you, the magnetic north can have some very strange effects. Just as well we have some supplies. We'll have to light a fire for cooking,' said Sionan, as he set about unpacking some firewood which he'd had the foresight to bring along. He proceeded to build a fire, then looked for the means to light it.

'I can light it,' said Olga.

'I'm sure you can, my Angel, just as soon as I find the matches.'

'No, I don't need matches. Watch!' said Olga, staring intensely at the base of the fire. As she stared, a red glow appeared under it, and within seconds it burst into flames.

'Wow! What's all that about, Olga? More magic? This gets crazier every minute!' Yiptop exclaimed, in complete amazement.

'Sure that will be the Moon magic! You'll surprise us with more of that as time goes by, I'll not doubt.'

'I just knew I could do that! I don't know why – something's happened with my eyes! I can see fine, but they feel different, as if they aren't just for seeing any more,' said Olga.

'Sure that's how my magic came to me. You get the idea you can do something, and then you try it and find that you can. You will also get some ideas and find that you can't. I spent about a year and gained a lot of bruises, sure that I could fly. Nearest I got was being very good at falling off walls,' said Sionan, with a smile.

Olga was playing with her new toy, staring at large chunks of ice and carving patterns in them. 'This is great, if we do save the Earth, I can become an ice sculptress. How cool is that?' said Olga, chuffed with her new ability.

'I'm sure you'd make a great ice sculptress, Olga, but somehow I think fate may have other things in store for your future,' Sionan said.

Yiptop was still very concerned with his apparent loss of contact with the LIC. Being not of this planet, he felt very insecure being out of contact with his means of returning home. He was checking the teleport unit.

'You pick a strange time to be doing your accounts, Yiptop. I take it you don't want to die in debt,' said Sionan,

Yiptop as usual looked completely puzzled at Sionan's humour. He was never really sure if he was serious or not.

'You're joking, right?' said Yiptop, straight faced.

'Well, sort of. I am wondering what you're doing with that calculator, though,' said Sionan.

Yiptop explained to Sionan what the teleporter was about. Sionan expressed the same reservations as Olga had.

Yiptop managed again in the same way to convince Sionan that it was a good idea.

'At least the teleporter is functioning correctly. I've run a full test on it,' Yiptop said.

'Sure by the sound of it, I hope we never need it. I can't say I fancy being de-materialised,' said Sionan.

'Nor me,' Olga added.

They settled down to eat their meal and drink some water, which Olga amused herself by providing from melted ice. Olga and Sionan decided to sleep and Yiptop needed his rest. They retired to the tent and for a few hours.

Their peace was broken after an hour by a tear appearing across the side of the tent, followed by a huge razor-clawed paw and a fiercely growling white head intruding into the tent. Sionan launched himself at the polar bear with incredible agility for one of his size, gripping the massive bear's throat with his hands. As the bear fell backwards under Sionan's weight his claws tore into his back like several sharp knives tearing into him as they wrestled on the ice. Sionan pulled his head back away from the beast who was trying to bite at his face. They thrashed around on the ice and snow, which was now becoming more and more red with Sionan's blood, pouring from the dreadful wounds on his back. Yiptop and Olga could only look on in horror. Olga was trying to burn her eyes into the great bear in an effort to help, but it was hopeless – the bear was moving too fast and it was impossible to focus on him. Prudence was standing near looking for an opportunity to get into the fight. Sionan brought his knees up into the belly of the bear and thrust him away will all the force his weakened body could muster. This gave him time to pull from his belt a long knife which glistened in the sunlight as he circled the bear, stabbing at his throat and body. Sionan cut and thrust at the animal, drawing blood at each vicious stab. The bear was now half white, half red from its own wounds.

Prudence barked and growled, still concentrating, waiting for the chance to attack. Olga's face was white with shock and fear as she saw the terrible wounds in Sionan's back. Prudence saw her chance as the bear held its head back in preparation for another attack on Sionan who was now barely standing. She leapt at the bear's throat with her wide mouth open, striking hard, pushing the animal onto its back, and twisting her head to do maximum damage, in an attempt to finish the fight. The bear recovered sufficiently to throw Prudence off.

Sionan was slowing down and hadn't much fight left in him. He had lost a great deal of blood and this was starting to drain the life from him. Prudence saw another chance and attacked again, striking at the throat with the same tactic, tearing and yanking at the throat, worsening the wound already inflicted in the previous onslaught. Once more the bear managed to throw Prudence off. This time it looked as if the bear could be fatally wounded. Arterial blood was pumping from the dreadful tear that Prudence had opened on her second attack. The bear was not going to last long. Sionan sadly looked no better. He staggered to one knee, still facing the bear, knife held up towards him, still losing blood from the wounds in his back.

The bear, still growling loudly, had had enough. He turned and walked away, hoping to die with some dignity, away from his fatal encounter with what he had initially regarded as today's meal. The crisis over, Sionan allowed himself to collapse face down in the snow, his motionless body looking limp and almost lifeless. Olga and Yiptop rushed over to him.

The Polar bear managed to put about a half a mile between them before blackness took over. His last thoughts were for his young, waiting for his return and the food that his kill would have provided for their survival.

A small band of Inuit stumbled on the dead polar bear.

'Namiq, namiq, ulu ga!' said Vaa.

In his language, a modern melange of Aleut and Yupik, he was saying 'polar bear, killed with a knife'. This was an unusual sight. In this sparsely populated area, nothing happened that Vaa didn't know about. Polar bears were virtually never killed, and certainly never with a knife, nor with their throats bitten with teeth marks that he didn't recognise.

'Iglu ptin ni !' said Vaa, indicating that the bear should be taken to his home for further inspection. He stood and looked all around him. 'Uman!' he called into the distance, calling the unseen one. 'Hakan!' – the one up high.

Vaa and his people took the great bear beck to their home. They were excited and puzzled at what was happening. Deeply superstitious and also at one with their environment, these people had been expecting this sign, mentioned in a legend that went back further in their history than any other. Back to the beginning.

'He's alive, but I don't know for how long,' said Yiptop.

'Sionan! Speak to me, Sionan! You can't die! We need you! You can't die!' Olga was screaming, tears running down her face.

'Angel,' said Sionan, 'the great bear's done for me. I'll not be going any further on this journey. Don't you worry for me, the Gods will look out for Sionan and see me into the next world. Go on and finish the job.' Sionan's voice was weak and barely audible.

Olga stood up to her full height, hands in the air, fingers stretched out.

'No!' she shouted, in the loudest voice she could manage. 'No, you will not die! I will not have you die, the Moon will not have you die. We have work to do and we will finish it together.'

Olga was shouting with rage, still standing with her arms outstretched, pointing to the sky. Shafts of deep, rich blue light, unlike any blue seen before, radiated from her fingers. Her hands and arms glowed with the same rich blue light. Olga thrust her hands down towards Sionan – he was now bathed in this same rich blue light. His whole body started to glow and lifted an inch or two from the ground. As his body lifted it became encapsulated in the glowing blueness and he started shivering from head to foot.

Olga clenched her fists and dropped her arms to her side. With that, Sionan fell to the ground, face down. Not one mark remained on his back – it was as if he had never fought the mighty polar bear. He started to move and rolled over onto his back.

'Sure you brought me back, my Angel! I don't know how, but that's some magic you have there.' He threw his arms open and Olga rushed to hug him, tears in her eyes, her face paled and drawn from the great energy she had summoned to save the giant.

'I had to save you, Sionan! I knew I could.'

'I have to admit, I thought that was the end of me, sure I did,' said Sionan, his voice back to its normal, resounding depth.

'I thought it was the end of all of us!' said Yiptop.

'You said an iceberg can spoil your whole day – I think a polar bear could spoil your whole week!' said Yiptop in an attempt at a humour he was never going to grasp.

Prudence joined in, licking everyone sloppily in the face.

'You brave dog, Prudence! You sent the nasty bear away,' said Olga, hugging the dog.

CHAPTER FIFTEEN

They took a couple of hours to recover from the shock. Olga felt quite unwell from the energy she had consumed in saving Sionan.

'Do you think that's part of my magic, or did the moon do that?' Olga asked.

'Good question, my Angel. It's hard to say if any magic is ours or if it just comes through us from the gods. I'm not sure it matters, I don't have much doubt that you will continue to have the use of your healing power,' Sionan replied.

'Cool, I can make people better!'

'Sure now that's going to be the hard part, especially for one so young,' Sionan said, looking pensive.

'How do you mean, how can it be hard making people better?'

'I'm sure that you're about to realise it any minute, but I'll tell you anyway. This world is not ready for it – if you turn up and start curing people all over the place, you will upset the balance of things. We live in a world where a scientific explanation is required for everything. This is because people are not courageous enough to accept. They need to hang an explanation label on everything. Some will treat you as a goddess, others will treat you as a witch. Some will believe that your power comes from an evil force. There will even be those who would abuse your power and try to gain power through you.

'Like me, you will need to learn the utmost discretion and keep your powers circumspect, not just for your own protection, but for the protection of all those who are not ready for you. This means that you will have to watch people suffer, knowing that you could do something, yet are unable to act for the risk of exposure. Also, if as we suspect, our powers are of the gods, then we have a responsibility of non-interference, except when we have genuine belief that it would be the wishes of the Gods that we interfere. With power comes responsibility. The greater the power, the greater the responsibility.'

'I hope I'm able to be strong enough,' said Olga, soberly.

'Don't you worry yourself about that until you're older. I won't be far away, and when we have seen the Air, provided all is well, you will have greater understanding.'

'Thanks, Sionan!' Olga smiled warmly.

Yiptop and Sionan had finished repairing the tent and were packing everything back onto the sleds.

'We'd best be moving on. We don't know how far the Air would have us walk,' said Sionan.

'Are you sure you don't want me to pull that sled?'
Yiptop offered.

'Sure I'm as right as rain, Yiptop. Whatever Olga did, it's as if I never got hurt.'

Meanwhile, Vaa and his family had arrived at their village, and his two elder sons were preparing to skin the great bear. Vaa was in his igloo with his eldest daughter Hmk. Vaa was the eldest of the group of Inuit which numbered in total seventy – which was unusual, as such groups normally numbered upwards of two hundred. But this was no ordinary Inuit community. Vaa's community were a mix of Siberian Yupik, and northeast Alaskan Mackenzie. They were well aware of their uniqueness, and believed strongly in their purpose, which was steeped in legend and history. A private community, they maintained strictly their purity of race, in which there was not an ounce of racist elitism. Their respect for others was paramount in their philosophy. Their function, which they valued above their own individual lives, was for the benefit of all people. They were the protectors of the domain of the Air. Their function and life work was to protect the domain of the Air from the interference of man.

They believed in education – in each generation, one person was selected and sent into the world. Vaa's daughter, Hmk, had been educated in Copenhagen, then she had then gone to Cambridge, where her PhD paper was a view of the socio-economic dichotomy in world ecology one hundred years from now. Hmk was fluent in three Latin languages and one Germanic, as well as her own Inuit language and dialects. Her function within the group was education, along with her elders and one junior of the same selection. They had a history that spanned many hundreds of millennia and the pinnacle of their belief was that Hakan would one day come for conference with the Uman. Hakan was the one from above, the one, of their people, who would return to them from the stars. Uman was the unseen one – the Air.

As their history told them, in the early days of their people, there came upon them a visit from the stars. Ten people were taken to populate a new world, a world close to theirs. These visitors taught them much about wisdom and understanding, and about what they called the proper order. They were told of the Moon and the Air, of the trees and residuals, and of the failings and inherent weaknesses of man. They were told of universal continuance. They were told that if man ever threatened universal continuance, the Moon would no longer beam, and in time the Air would leave and this world would end. They were also told that one chance of survival would be offered, and that with this chance, Hakan would come – one of their people returning in their hour of need. It was more than thirty years since the Moon had stopped beaming. The air was becoming all but unbreathable, and even within their own people, creativity had diminished to unrecognizable levels.

They had been waiting for this day and Vaa was sure that it had now arrived. Speaking to Hmk, he insisted that the time had come, and that Hakan would come any day now. Vaa was not a select educate, and his education and knowledge was far below that of Hmk, but his daughter understood well that knowledge and understanding, though often complementary, were not at all interchangeable. After long discussion, she bowed to his superior wisdom and agreed that his insight was secure and that indeed Hakan was close and would be with them soon. So Vaa and his people were preparing for the arrival, with scouts all over the area looking for Hakan.

'Sure it's the strangest feeling I've felt in a long time,' said Sionan.

'What feeling is that?' Yiptop responded.

'I feel it too,' said Olga.

'Will one of you stop being so obtuse and tell me what you're talking about?' Yiptop said, frustrated at living with the newly interconnected magicians, as he privately considered them, though he had great respect for them.

'We're in the middle of a very sparsely populated area, and we should feel very alone, yet we are being watched and followed,' said Sionan.

'So what do we do?' Yiptop asked.

'When you play chess, you anticipate problems that may occur by studying the other players' options and thinking them through to their possible conclusions, but you can't make the other players move for them, you have to wait. So, we consider the possibilities, but for whoever is watching, it's their move,' Sionan answered.

'So, once more, we just wait...' said Yiptop, very much a person of action.

'Yiptop, people of action, like yourself, often fail to realise that calculated inaction is, in itself, action,' Sionan commented.

In this vast wilderness it would be easy to see other travellers, if they were close enough to see you. Well, that was the very thought Sionan was considering when Vaa and Hmk appeared in front of them. They stood in blank amazement to find two people who had somehow managed with alarming deftness to appear a few feet in front of them without prior warning.

'By what magic do you appear in front of us like that, and what is your purpose?' Sionan said in his no-nonsense tone.

Just as Sionan said that, Olga and Yiptop were in joint fly-catching mode, mouths wide open.

'Do you see what I see, Yiptop?' said Olga in a whispered aside.

'Depends what you see, but probably.'

'Are you from Zog?' said Olga, this time loud enough for everyone to hear.

'Hakan, Hakan!' said Vaa, looking both shocked and delighted, and very much like Yiptop.

'It's true – you are Hakan! You must be Hakan,' said Hmk to Yiptop.

Then turning to Sionan she said, 'Forgive me – I forget my manners. I am Hmk and this is my father Vaa. Our purpose is the very same as yours. My people have inhabited this land for millennia. We can move without being seen – no magic, it is a skill.'

'Good to meet you. I am Sionan, Spirit of Leprechaun.'

Sionan introduced the others. Vaa and Hmk bowed to them, and for want of the right etiquette they all bowed back, except of course Prudence, who barked approvingly.

'Please come with us to our home. All will be explained. We know that you are here for the Air, so please trust us,' said Hmk.

Olga turned to Sionan, 'She's speaking the truth, I know it.'

'And I know it too.' Sionan turned to Hmk and Vaa. 'We will follow you,' He said.

They followed for nearly two hours and arrived at the Igloo village. Food and refreshments were laid on and everyone seemed to be interested in Yiptop and were all talking about him. Olga didn't understand their language, but Yiptop was quite obviously the focus of attention.

'This is crazy,' said Yiptop, in another aside to Olga. 'My sister is called Hmk and I have an uncle called Vaa. In fact most people at home do – it's the most common name on Zog.'

'They look so much like you,' said Olga.

They went into one of the many Igloos with Vaa and Hmk leaving Prudence outside with the sleds.

Hmk spoke first. 'We are the people of the Air; our place is to protect the domain of the Air.'

'Cool,' said Olga. 'But why do you look so much like Yiptop?' She pointed to Yiptop with her thumb as he sat next to her.

'It is not we who look like him, but more he who looks like us. I will explain,' said Hmk.

Hmk explained how, in ancient times, ten of their people were taken to populate a nearby planet. She explained also that they knew, although they didn't know exactly why, about the Moon problem, and that it must be that man had compromised universal continuance.

'But your names?' said Yiptop. 'They are names from Zog.'

'No,' said Hmk. 'Once again, your names on Zog are from here.'

'So I am of your people!' said Yiptop incredulously.

'Yes, you are Hakan, the one from above, the one we have know throughout history would come with others to seek the last salvation of this world.'

At this Vaa stood up and bowed, saying 'Hakan'.

'This is all a bit of a shocking revelation!' Yiptop said, looking quite overwhelmed. 'The people of my planet bear a direct relation to your people. We are equally descendents of your ancients, as you are!'

'Yes, of course. We are cousins,' said Hmk

Vaa had no English, only his own language. He communicated through Hmk, expressing his delight that the Gods had chosen to bring this about during his lifetime. He expressed how his people had spent the last thirty years or so almost in despair, knowing that the end could be soon, but at the same time confident in their faith that Hakan would come and with him bring hope for survival. The atmosphere became more relaxed and comfortable and they all ate the wonderful food provided. They met all seventy or so of these Yiptop lookalikes.

Tiredness was overcoming them. They were taken to a large Igloo to rest, and Hmk and Vaa left them alone for a few hours, wisely suggesting that time for reflection was needed for all.

'This is certainly not a twist I was expecting,' said Sionan.

'I knew there had to be more than just coincidental reasons for your appearance, Yiptop,' Olga said.

'I sort of thought that something was drawing me inexorably deeper into this affair, but I had no idea what.' Yiptop still looked shocked. 'There are legends that my people were brought to Zog by the gods, and that we did not evolve by normal evolutionary process. No-one however thought that we could have come from Earth. It makes no sense. How could we have made so much progress, while you Earth people have made so little?' he said.

'Sure now take it easy with the poor backward Earth people bit. I've got feelings, you know. Anyhow, as far as I can see, all you've got is more toys than us!' Sionan said indignantly.

'It is possible that our developments have differed and that we have things to teach each other. Certainly Zog has greater technological advancement,' said Olga.

'Yes, and you still have magic.'

'I am not at all surprised,' said Sionan.

'You're not?' said Yiptop and Olga in unison.

'Not at all at all,' said Sionan. 'I was fairly sure that there would be people who would protect the domain of the Air. I was equally sure that you,' he looked at Yiptop, 'had a deeper involvement in all of this. I am also sure that there will have been much exchange of people between planets, and some of it at the behest of the gods. After all, the Gods created life, so it's reasonable that despite non-interference, the Gods might make changes if they see an overwhelming reason.'

'It seems clear to me that whatever the Air has in mind, you, Yiptop, will form a big part of it,' said Olga.

They rested for a few hours, Olga slept and so did Sionan for a short time.

They were getting closer to the air by the minute and had yet to find out what they must go through, but the time seemed to be coming.

CHAPTER SIXTEEN

Olga was invited into Hmk's igloo, while Sionan and Yiptop were taken to speak with the other select educates.

'Olga, tell me how your part in all this came about,' said Hmk.

'It all really started when I was walking home from school, on a Thursday afternoon. Although I had already met Yiptop a few weeks before that.'

Olga went on to tell Hmk the whole story of the post, the stones, the Grain of Truth, Prudence, Sionan, and how her special powers seemed to be developing. She also tried to explain how her mind had started to develop very rapidly, as if preparing her for something. Hmk was astonished at Olga's grasp of concepts and her articulation in explaining such complex issues.

'How do you feel, Olga, about being Angel of the Moon, and not just little old Olga?' Hmk asked.

'I haven't really had much time to think about it in that way. I've thought quite a lot about things that the stones and Sionan have told me, about the proper order of things. I've thought about continuance and the way the world seems to work and I think I sort of understand why it must be that way. But, I haven't really given much thought to how I *feel* about it. I'm not sure there is much point. I am Angel of the Moon, I can't change it. I could have been much worse things, but what I suppose I really mean is, I don't think I could have been much *better* things. Now that you've got me thinking about it, and assuming for a minute that the world will be able to continue, I think being Angel of the Moon is just about the coolest thing ever imaginable,' Olga replied, visibly lightening at having thought about it.

'You don't resent it at all? The normality of your childhood is probably gone forever. It is unlikely that you will be on the same wavelength as most of your school friends.'

'No way! Since I took the Grain, and that was about nine years ago, I haven't been on the same wavelength as anyone, but I can reach their wavelength and people can reach mine. My friend Emily, who I miss loads by the way, understands a lot about me. She knows nothing about all of this, but she knows me, and I know her.'

'You seem to be very accepting.'

'I don't see the point in not accepting. Things have a habit of carrying on, fairly disregarding your protests. Anyway, I think we really only have a say in the small things – the big things seem to run themselves. Having said that, small things can make a huge difference. I think it's fun being Olga and being Angel of the Moon at the same time.'

'I can see what you mean.'

'What do you think, Hmk? Do you think we will succeed in whatever the Air wants of us?' Olga asked, adeptly turning the interview around, not something Hmk failed to notice.

'Olga, you really are very special – if anyone can do it, you can. For what it's worth, I think, you, with Yiptop and Sionan, will save us all somehow. Failure has a peculiar smell about it, and I don't smell it around this.'

'Hmk, this might sound a bit silly, but I'd like you to explain something to me. Sionan started to tell me about this guy called Fibonnany or something, and another guy called Loo Tsy. It was when we were passing the icebergs – it seemed relevant to the icebergs, but he didn't finish explaining. You know what it's like when someone half tells you something? It's been really bugging me.'

'I think you mean Fibonacci and Lao Tzu.'

'Yes, them! What are they all about?'

'I can sympathise with Sionan for not finishing. Talking about these two people in anything but a superficial way requires first a conceptual shift, which in most people is hard to achieve. Let's look at that shift first.'

'Do you mean an extension in my conceptual parameters?' said Olga.

'Well, Olga! That's precisely what I mean! But how do you know that at ten years old?'

'I did conceptual parameters with Yiptop when we were watching a sunrise,' said Olga.

'Okay then, see if you understand this. You like music and art?'

'Yes.'

'Why do you like music and art? Is it just that music sounds pleasant, and great paintings look pretty?'

'No, it's much more than that. Music and art touch me in a way that other things can't.'

'Yes, but why?'

'Not sure, but they do.'

'It's to do with direct sensory access. For example, a great artist might paint a picture of a field of bluebells. When you look at the painting you don't just see the field of bluebells. In fact, visually, it might even be a very inaccurate representation of that field of bluebells. What the artist will do is produce a painting that will evoke in you just how the field of bluebells made him feel. To do that, it may be that visually, the painting has little or no need to look like the physical thing it represents. That's because it is about evoking an emotion.'

'Like Jackson Pollock?'

'Olga, I am impressed! That's a perfect example.'

'I like Jackson Pollock.'

'And you like him because he can change the way you feel, not just make a pretty picture for you to look at.'

'Yes, and great music does the same, it goes direct and opens a door to something.'

'Yes. That's the conceptual shift, from the physical to the metaphysical.'

'I've got that, but what's it got to do with Fibonacci and the other guy?'

'A little at a time and we will get there. Hold on to what we just talked about while I tell you a bit about Fibonacci. Fibonacci was an Italian mathematician, also known as Leonardo of Pisa. He is responsible for a massive departure in thinking. Many people still haven't realised quite how important he was and wouldn't place him among people like Da Vinci or Einstein. I think that is because they haven't seen the enormity of it. I would place him up there with the greatest minds ever, although it's not a race. The reason is that he actually made mathematical sense of part of that conceptual shift and furthered our understanding of it, and he also related it to creation itself, and therefore to the Gods themselves.'

'This is really cool! How did he do that?'

'With numbers, as you would expect from a mathematician.'

'Tell me! I'm really into this.' Olga was getting very excited.

'As you were passing the icebergs did you know that they were two thirds under water and one third above?'

'Yes, Sionan told me that.'

'Did you also know that this planet's surface is two thirds water and one third land, and that you are two thirds water and one third other stuff?'

'I do now.'

'Well, it's not exactly a ratio of two thirds and one third, but that's not so important, and it is very close to that. What's interesting is that as well as that approximate ratio, there are other important ratios, all of which relate to the way we perceive things – not just visually, but in all ways. Fibonacci realised this, and as a mathematician does, he got to work with numbers. He took one and two and put them together to get three.'

'No flies on him, then!' Olga said laughing.

'Then he took two and three to get five, then three and five to get eight, then five and eight to get thirteen. An infinite sequence of numbers, obtained by adding the successive number to the previous, became what he called the Golden Numbers. This may sound a bit strange – he didn't just play around with numbers to get this sequence, not any more than Jackson Pollock just randomly threw paint at the canvas. He knew he was onto something big. He realised that these numbers gave him the universal ratios of creation itself, a direct link to understanding creation, the universe, us, our perception, the gods, everything. 'Anything that we like, visually, will connect in some way to these ratios. The relationship between our bone sizes and the proportions in the make-up of our bodies and faces, they also follow these ratios. When nature produces plants, trees animals, and insects, it would seem that it follows these golden ratios. Look at art, sculpture, the way in which we construct music, both melodically and rhythmically, even the way in which a tempered scale is produced. Look at the universe in macro and micro, that's big and small, look at the way planets moons and suns relate, then look at the way, on a subatomic level, that electrons neutrons and protons relate. All of everything is based on these numbers. Even the ratio of hours we sleep and wake, even the way our concentration works, the way our memories work, the way we naturally set up time spans. We haven't even begun to explore the staggering enormity of Fibonacci's work. The observations of Fibonacci are the very tools which give us calculable access to the very roots, the foundations, of nature and creation.'

'Cool. And what about Lao Tzu?' said Olga, who at the moment just couldn't get enough. Her mind was vacuous for knowledge and information.

'Lao Tzu was a philosopher – Chinese non-causal.'

'But what was special about him? Sionan wouldn't have mentioned him if he wasn't at least as special as Fibonacci.'

'Oh, he was special, so special that it would take a year or so just to tell you about him.'

'But tell me something! I must know something, then I'll find out more.'

'I'll try... Lao Tzu had an incredible insight into the loose yet perceptible relationship that absolutely everything has with absolutely everything else. He talked about it all being about changes. In fact he was pivotal in the creation of the Book of Changes. This book is known as the *I Ching*, the sacred Taoist oracle of changes. This is certainly one of the most important books ever written. It has been said by many scholars, both ancient and modern, that this book contains the sum total of human wisdom.'

'But can such ancient wisdom apply to our times?'

'Olga, your ability to understand shocks me sometimes, but as a ten-year-old, I suppose it is good to see that you still have some naivety. Wisdom is not a thing of time or place nor can it be superseded by knowledge. True wisdom is forever. It owes nothing to the changeable props of modern life.'

'Sorry, I'm only ten.'

'I know. That's okay… Lao Tzu was also instrumental in the creation of the *Tao Te Ching*, which means the way and the virtue of change. Another of the most important books ever. The *I Ching* was used throughout its history as an instrument of divination.'

'What's divination?'

'Well, literally it's guessing, but more realistically it's about predicting the outcome of certain situations by understanding how the situation sits within the current change system operating. It's not simple, but it's very much worthy of considerable study.'

'I will – I will do all of these things… but first we have to save the world!'

'But more importantly than anything else, never lose sight of the very great difference between wisdom, understanding, and knowledge – never confuse them, they are truly not interchangeable.'

'I'll always try to remember that.'

'Good. When all this is over, we'll spend time together. I will be there with Sionan to help with your study.'

'But how? When this is over, I'll have to go home to my parents, and my friends and my school.'

'Of course, and you will. It is I, Sionan and hopefully Yiptop, who will displace ourselves to be near you, and it is together that we will do the great work needed, to set things right and realign this world with the proper order of things.'

'This sounds so cool.'

'Olga, you have an incredible capacity to take so much in your stride. But now, we must rejoin the others and get this business resolved.'

'I know. But Hmk, will you and Vaa come with us to meet the Air?'

'That isn't possible Olga. We haven't been summoned. The Air wants you, Hakan – or Yiptop as you know him – Sionan, and Prudence. The Air has asked for no other, and it would be most imprudent to make any changes.'

By the time Olga and Hmk joined the others, they had prepared everything for departure. Prudence was harnessed, and they were ready to leave. Yiptop was impatient, as usual.

'Come on, Olga!' he said. 'We must go. We still don't know how far we will need to travel.'

They all said their goodbyes and moved off northwards to who knows where.

CHAPTER SEVENTEEN

Emily was in the hospital. It was one of many appointments during which they had poked around in her ears and did what they could to restore her hearing. So far it had all been in vain, and Emily was still profoundly deaf. Not only deaf, but also angry, and as yet, not at all adjusted to her situation. She was frustrated with the practicalities of trying to somehow know what people wanted to say to her – not knowing how to lip-read, she was obliged to read written messages. Already her voice was becoming louder, as she had no way of knowing the required volume to speak.

Her parents were still distraught. They were angry too, more angry than Emily. Their anger was based on one of the most fundamental principles of all life – continuance. A parent's love for their child is so enormous and basic that it can really only be understood by a parent. Even then, perhaps only by a parent who has faced the loss or near-loss of their child. The offspring of any sentient is their immortality, their own continuance, the whole reason and purpose for their existence, written deeply within their very being. People are programmed to survive and protect themselves for the sake of their own temporary continuance, a threat towards a child threatens even more, it threatens immortality, peoples overall continuance.

Emily was not at risk of dying; she was healthy and well, but she had been damaged and it seemed probable she would always be impaired. Her parents were indeed grateful that in every other way she was fine. They were however deeply aggrieved for what had been taken from her.

'I wish Olga was here, and not on holiday in Portugal,' said Emily.

Emily's mum typed all her replies on a laptop computer which they had brought into the hospital especially for that purpose.

'She'll be back in a couple of days, darling. School will be starting,' Emily's mum typed.

'Yes, but I won't be able to go to school, will I? I'll have to go to some special school for people who can't hear. I won't know anyone there and I won't be in class with Olga. We do everything together. I wish we hadn't had that dreadful crash with those stupid boys.'

'So do I, my darling. The good news is that you can go back to your own school for the time being. There is a chance, Emily. If they do this operation they think it may be possible to restore a little bit of hearing in one ear.'

'I don't like operations. It's all very scary.'

'It'll be fine, darling. You'll be asleep, and it won't hurt. We must try.'

'You're right, Mum. Olga would be brave. She's always brave.'

'Darling, as soon as Olga's back, we'll bring her to see you. But now, you should get some sleep, because they want to operate in the morning.'

Emily lay down in her hospital bed by the window and tried to get off to sleep.

Northwards they went through this frozen wasteland. It was some days since they had seen night. At this time of year, night and day were the same white snow-blinding scene. In diffused light, there were no distinct sharp edges to focus on, in fact nothing for the eyes to fix on at all, no variation. The eyes just stared unfocused at the bland white nothingness, unable to fix on any point, unable to make perspective sense of distance and scale. Were it not for the special capacities of our team, they would not have survived this far, such was the extreme inhospitality of this place, the place the Air called home.

After eight long hours of travel, they stopped to set up camp. Sionan and Yiptop put the tent together and Olga lit a fire in her inimitable way. They settled down to eat the fish, which had been prepared and provided by their new Inuit friends.

'Sionan, why d'you think the Air is making us walk so far? It helped us through the pack ice by lifting us onto the clouds, and now we're left to walk all this way. It doesn't make a whole lot of sense,' said Olga.

'That's true, I was wondering that as well,' Yiptop added.

'I'm not sure I have the answer. Maybe there was an insurmountable problem at Baffin Bay which the Air knew we would never overcome – it is a bit early in the year. And now perhaps the Air is testing our resolve,' Sionan replied.

'I'm not sure that's it. Who knows? I'm a bit worried about more polar bears. Do you think we might see more?' Olga nervously asked Sionan.

'I certainly hope not, but this is their home, so it's possible,' Sionan said, being honest but at the same time trying not to cause alarm.

'As I don't need sleep, I could keep a watch while you two sleep,' said Yiptop, ever practical.

'I have a feeling that won't be necessary. Can you feel the way that wind is developing?' said Sionan.

'Yes, I can,' said Yiptop, 'and it is starting to snow.'

The wind was starting up in short but powerful gusts. Snow was being driven along with it, both new falling snow and dry surface snow.

'With a snow storm brewing, the last thing we need to worry about right now is polar bears. They'll be dug in to sit out the storm, which is exactly what we should be doing.'

'I suppose that's some good news then,' said Olga, cheerfully.

'It may be, as long as we get started with digging ourselves in right now.' Sionan went to the sleds and got two shovels. 'We need a hole about two feet deep and big enough to get us and everything else in, and we need it fast.'

They dug for nearly two hours. Mercifully the storm, though well on its way, had not yet taken hold fully. Sionan took the tent down and laid it in the hole like a sort of large sleeping bag. He placed the two sleds at either end of the hole and signalled Prudence to lie down against one of them. The three of them then got into the tent as if it were a large bed.

'We stay here till this storm blows itself out. By the time it does, we'll be under a few feet of snow,' said Sionan, as the wind and accompanying snow were becoming more and more violent.

'Will we be able to breathe if we're covered with snow? Breathing would be preferable,' said Yiptop.

'You'll not need to worry about that. Sure I have done this before, you know,' said Sionan, holding some very strange-looking metal tubes. 'See these tubes? They'll give us air when we're covered in snow,' Sionan said reassuringly.

'This is quite cosy,' said Olga.

'It's not my idea of cosy, but I do appreciate your positivism, Olga!'

They were all huddled in the hole – about the safest way to be, for what they were about to encounter. As the storm progressed, they were gradually becoming, completely covered in snow. Not exactly comfortable, but well-protected from the elements' apparent desire to destroy them. As the snow covering thickened above them, Sionan was skilfully working at the inner surface, pushing and packing the snow up against the weight of the snow above them, creating a dome-like air space which allowed some movement. As his work progressed, their dug-out developed into a sort of closed tunnel, with about eighteen inches of space above them.

Despite his huge bulk, Sionan showed nimbleness in a tight

space, which was quite incongruous. Within this tight space,

Sionan put together a series of interlocking tubes. The top had

a domed shape, to prevent it from filling with snow as it was

pushed upwards towards the surface, providing them with air

while they waited it out. The vicious sound of the storm had

subsided to a whisper, as a result of the insulating effect of the

snow. Outside of their small cocooned world, the scene had

become one of such violence that they would not have

survived minutes of it, even with their special strengths and

powers. Visibility was virtually down to zero. The combined

power of wind and dry snow was acting like a vicious iced

sand blaster, powerful and cold enough to tear flesh from

bone. It was impossible to breathe the cold, snow-ridden, fast-

moving air, and impossible to even stand in the violent wind;

they would have perished on the spot.

'Where did you learn these things, Sionan?' said Yiptop, in awe of Sionan's apparent genius.

'Sure you pick these things up along the way,' said Sionan nonchalantly.

'How will we know when the storm is over? It's difficult to hear anything.' Olga asked, pertinently.

'You just wait and see! I have that sorted as well,' Sionan replied, as he assembled another set of interlocking tubes which had string running through the middle. He pushed it through the snow and pulled the string, releasing a cap from the top. This exposed a vane which started to spin in the wind, a duplicate of which spun before them at the inner end of the tube.

'When that stops spinning, the storm is over,' said Sionan, satisfied with his work.

'Even more brilliant!' said Yiptop, a great lover of gadgets at the best of times.

'There's no more we can do now, so we may as well rest. These storms can last hours, even days,' said Sionan.

They rested, safe and cocooned as the storm raged above them. They lost all sense of time during the five hours that the storm prevailed.

'Look,' said Yiptop. 'It's stopped spinning!'

Sionan checked that the vane was not blocked by manually turning the inner end of it.

'Sure enough, it's over,' said Sionan.

He removed the tubes and in the process ascertained that they were under about four feet of snow. Suddenly and dramatically, with one almighty heave of his huge body, Sionan stood upright, clearing almost all the snow in his wake.

'Sionan, you look like a polar bear,' laughed Olga.

Prudence jumped out of the snow and began running in circles, excited at his release. They spent the next hour or two clearing snow from the sleds and putting the tent away.

They moved on. The snow was newly soft and deep, their feet sinking several inches with every step, even in their snowshoes. This made hard work of walking.

'The going gets tough,' Sionan commented.

'And the tough get going,' Olga replied, laughing.

'Sure you're happy enough for a little ten-year-old, in a life-threatening situation, my Angel,' said Sionan, affectionately.

'Yes the closer we get to the air, the happier I am, and something tells me we're very close,' said Olga.

'I'm sure I won't argue with you, but I think we could still have a way to go. Sionan responded.

'It still puzzles me that the Air is putting us through this,' said Olga.

'Me too,' said Yiptop.

'I'm not so sure it's fair to say the Air is putting us through this. Maybe it's just that the Air is not helping as much as it could.'

'No, Sionan, I don't agree,' said Olga, firmly. 'The wind is the Air, and we just had a snow storm that was the direct work of the Air, any way you look at it.'

'All we can do is go on,' Sionan said, resignedly.

'The more I think about it, something's not right. I feel we're nearly there and yet I feel there's something in our way, something in the air. At one point, we seemed to be welcomed and getting help, but since we left Vaa and Hmk, we seem to be getting hindered. There's something in our way, but I don't know what it is,' said Olga.

'I do!' said Yiptop, barely able to get the words out.

'No! Please, someone – tell me I'm not seeing that!' Sionan said, looking into the near distance with disbelief.

'Oh, my god!' Olga exclaimed.

'Now what do we do?' said Yiptop.

'Sure if I knew I would tell you,' Sionan replied.

'What are they doing?' Olga asked.

'Stalking us is what they're doing, waiting for the right time to strike at us,' Sionan said, as Prudence seemed to be getting into attack mode. 'Prudence, stay close, girl!' he said firmly. 'I'm sure I can't fight five polar bears, but I'll sure enough have a go before I let us die here.'

Yiptop reached into his pocket and pulled out the teleporter.

'Time for a sharp exit, I think that's the saying,' he said.

'I won't be arguing with that,' said Sionan, relieved.

'No!' shouted Olga. 'No way!' She grabbed the teleporter from Yiptop's hand. 'This is our problem,' she said.

'No, Olga! That's our saviour! Don't do anything crazy!' Yiptop shouted.

'You're wrong! It's this that's stopping us,' said Olga.

The bears were moving in closer and surrounding them as they spoke. Prudence was getting very nervous, and her natural defensive aggression was kicking in. Olga pulled out the teleporter plug inscribed with her name, and threw it as far as she could into the distance.

'Olga, what have you done? That's crazy! It's our only way out of here,' Yiptop shouted.

Olga handed the teleporter back to Yiptop. Sionan remained quiet and pensive, as he generally did in the most difficult situations.

'I can't save us now!' said Yiptop.

'Don't you get it?' said Olga, calmly.

'I do,' said Sionan. 'And I think you could be right – it's a brave shout, to be sure!'

'Will someone please tell me what's going on, at least so I know it before I get eaten by one of those bears?' Yiptop pleaded.

'Look,' said Olga. 'They're going.'

'She's right! Well, will you look at that?' Sionan said in amazement.

The polar bears were now moving further and further away from them.

'Angel, sure you're as clever as a box of monkeys, you are! You see Yiptop, the Air is not a daft as us. The Air knew we had a way out. The Air knew that with your teleporter we had a back door to safety, and it needed to test our determination and will. Olga has proved she has the courage and the bare-faced wit for the job in hand.'

'So now what,' said Yiptop.

'So now we set up camp and wait. We've made our last move and the Air is in check. It is the Air's move now,' said Sionan.

Yiptop took the teleporter and threw the whole thing as far as he could. 'We're all in this together – make your move, Air!' he shouted.

CHAPTER EIGHTEEN

A strange and almost surreal mixture of calmness and excitement prevailed at the camp. The calmness came from the Air's intervention and the implication of its approval. The excitement came from anticipating the unknown that lay before them, and the knowledge that the end game was near. Exactly how near this end game was, only time would tell – seconds, minutes, hours? Who could say?

'Do you hear something?' asked Olga.

'Yes, something in the air,' said Yiptop.

'Sure, me too,' said Sionan.

They were sitting in the tent surrounded by a flat white wilderness of emptiness, stretching out as far as the ill-defined horizon that encircled them.

'It sounds a long way off, but getting nearer and louder,' said Olga.

'What is it?' Yiptop asked.

'Sounds like an orchestra and a choir,' said Olga.

'Sure, it's Beethoven, his ninth symphony, "Ode to Joy",' said Sionan, as he started singing along in German.

'I don't care if its Beethoven or Billy Idol – I meant what is it, as in, what are we doing hearing a full orchestra and choir out here on the polar ice cap?' Yiptop ranted.

'I don't think Billy Idol would be at all appropriate,' said Olga.

'I give up!' said Yiptop in despair.

The sound of a large orchestra and choir, conducted with the kind of astute sensitivity achieved only by a few great conductors, was indeed getting nearer and louder. It was also coming to an end, with massive applause and cheering from a very large audience.

'It's a live recording!' said Yiptop. 'What's anyone doing playing a live recording out here?'

'It's not a recording,' said a very loud voice that came not really from anywhere, but from everywhere.

'Who are you?' Yiptop asked.

'Shush, I haven't finished,' said the very loud voice.

A song started, this time not too loud, but very clear – as if the singer and his guitar were within a few yards of them.

'I love James Taylor!' Olga whispered. 'I love this song, too.'

'So we just sit and listen to the music?' whispered Yiptop.

'Yes,' Olga replied.

'If it's not a recording, what is it?' Yiptop said, slightly louder.

'It's live music,' said the voice. 'Now shush and listen.'

'I think we should all shut up and listen,' Sionan whispered.

They all sat calmly and in silence, enjoying James Taylor singing 'Shower the People' very simply and beautifully, just him and an old Martin guitar, meaning every word. When that finished, again to rapturous applause, some country music began – Dobro, fiddle, bass, and guitar. That too finished, this time to applause, shouting, and whistling.

'Any requests?' said the voice.

'Yes! Where's it coming from?' said Yiptop.

'The last one was from a small club in Nashville,' said the voice, 'But I meant any requests as in, is there anything you would like to hear?'

'Yes!' said Olga, 'Bette Midler singing "The Rose".'

'Sorry, she's asleep,' said the voice.

'What?' said Yiptop.

'She's asleep,' the voice repeated.

'Who's asleep?' Yiptop asked.

'Bette Midler,' The voice replied.

'This is nuts!' said Yiptop. 'Where is all this coming from?'

'All over the place,' said the voice. 'Now shush and listen to this. I've found something really lovely.'

A wonderful haunting melody played on some kinds of flutes surrounded them. They all listened, captivated by the simple beauty. It finished, and this time there was no applause.

'That wasn't live,' said Yiptop.

'Was,' said the voice.

'Where was the audience, then?' Yiptop asked.

'There was no audience. They were playing at their home in Bolivia,' said the voice.

'How are you doing this?' Yiptop asked.

'I'm not doing it,' said the voice.

'Well, who is?' said Yiptop.

'You had the London Symphony Orchestra, then James Taylor at a small venue in Maryland, then some musicians in Nashville. You couldn't have Bette Midler, because she was asleep and she doesn't generally sing in her sleep. Then you had two very wonderful young kena players accompanied by two people playing charango in Bolivia.

'So that's who – what about how, even maybe why?' said Yiptop.

Sionan remained in silent observation throughout.

'Okay. I'm sorry, I'll stop being silly now. It's just that we have such serious and important matters to deal with, I thought it would be nice to enjoy a little music together.'

'You like music then,' Sionan broke his silence.

'Like music! I *am* music, music is me. It was I who lay still in Grapelli's violin waiting to obey his commands, moving to his whim, making reality of his bow strokes, mirroring the verity of his intonation at the same time reflecting and responding to the phrases from Django's guitar. It is I who pass through the lungs of the greatest operatic singers – though sadly, also some of the worst. It is I who takes it to the ears of the audience, each individual one of them. Oh yes, I like music, I am music. But I am many things, I am the climate. I carry the rain, the clouds, I bring you warm and cold winds, even hurricanes. I am your hearing, your smell, every breath you take. I hold you all in my grasp, I love this planet like a mother loves her child. I have held you all in my arms since creation. I am the Air. Welcome, my friends.'

'Thank you,' said Olga. 'The music was lovely, and it was a lovely idea.'

'You liked it then,' said the Air.

'I loved it,' said Olga.

'I am pleased! I've never interacted with people in this way before. I hoped you would like music, it's my favourite thing,' said the Air.

'Beats polar bears and snow storms,' said Yiptop.

'Yiptop, don't be rude!' Olga snapped.

'Don't worry, I'm not offended easily; not much bothers me. I don't like aircraft breaking the sound barrier; they always catch me napping. Any sort of farting is most unpleasant, as are factories and motor cars, but I'm generally quite easygoing,' the Air assured them. 'Anyway, I'd better sort out some transport.'

'Where are we going?' Sionan asked.

'Yes, of course, forgive me if I drift off occasionally. I have things going on all over the planet. I have reserved enough consciousness for this, but I'm not really used to chatting, and I suppose I should admit I've been quite nervous about it. I have had time to prepare, so I've built a little housey thing with all the comforts you need. It will take an hour or so to get you there. A cloud will arrive shortly, so just pile onto it, sit comfortably and enjoy the ride.'

A small, pinkish white cloud, complete with silver lining, looking a bit like an open oyster shell filled with pink cotton wool, descended and parked itself in front of them.

'Is it there?' said the Air.

'Yes,' said Olga, 'it's here.'

'Good, good! Just jump on, with all your stuff and we can get going. Oh, by the way, are you all warm enough?'

'Sionan and I are using our magic to stay warm, Prudence seems fine, and Yiptop is good for a wide range of temperatures, beyond the scope of this planet,' Olga reported.

'You'll find the cloud very warm, and the housey thing. My little helpers will greet you on arrival, and see to anything you need. See you shortly, then. Ciao for now!' said the Air.

They pulled the sleds up onto the cloud, and Prudence jumped up and immediately sprawled luxuriously, then the rest got on.

'It's all soft and warm,' said Olga.

The pink cloud moved slowly up. Without reaching any great altitude, it began to move forward, rather in the way you would expect a magic carpet to behave. Their journey lasted just over an hour. On the white horizon they saw what would be best described as a castley thing, a sort of white fairy castle topped with icing sugar with large turrets at each side, one of them extending much higher than the others like a sort of watchtower. A drawbridge in the middle was lowering as they approached. The cloud slowed down, and descended to about two feet off the ground. To the right of the castley thing, in the distance, they could see a huge white tiger prowling like a huge wild cat and watching. Two riders were approaching, and the wind began to howl. The magnificence of this castle was spectacular. For Olga it evoked memories of every fairytale she'd ever heard, and as it happened, a song by Bob Dylan. For Sionan it brought to mind old Leprechaun stories, and for Yiptop, it put him in mind of ancient legends of magic. Each of them was in awe for their own reasons as they glided towards the castle gate on their warm, soft cloud. The cloud stopped. Two very short people, looking remarkably like miniature versions of Sionan and riding proportionally miniature white horses, turned out to be the riders who were approaching.

'Would you ever in your whole life believe it?' Sionan exclaimed. 'Leprechauns!'

Sionan jumped off the cloud and got down on his knees to greet them. 'Well hello, little fellas, what are you doing here? There are no more Leprechauns!'

'Respect and praise, Spirit of Leprechaun, we are sent from a far off planet at the request of the Gods themselves. We are here to serve the Air and your every need while you are here with the Air. I am Ned and this is Hamish,' said Ned.

'Sure is good to see you both! I never thought in my life I would ever see a Leprechaun. This is Olga, Angel of the Moon, Yiptop Hakan of Zog, and Prudence Spirit of Moondog.'

'Happy as a happy thing, to see you all,' said Hamish.

'Sure, I'm pleased as a plump pomegranate,' said Ned.

'Follow us,' said Hamish. 'The Air has taken a lot of trouble to ensure your comfort.'

Sionan jumped back up on the cloud and it followed behind the horsemen. As they glided through the castle gate, the white tiger came in behind them and climbed the ramparts, then remained out of sight.

'Leave all your things to us. You'll want to rest, and soon we'll all eat,' said Ned.

'Sure, and don't you be worrying, Sionan, we have the cold Guinness from the emerald Isle. We'll be sharing some of that together this day, to be sure,' said Hamish.

They all got off the cloud.

'Nice place,' said Olga.

Effectively, the castley thing was a gigantic igloo, although by some magic, much more sophisticated.

'It's all ice,' said Yiptop, 'but it has the texture and look of wood and stone and gold. This is really amazing!'

Ned and Hamish led them into the main building, down corridors with apparently wooden floors with semi-translucent stone-like walls and luminescent gold ceilings.

'It's like a magic grotto,' said Olga.

'Ned, myself, and the Air, have been working for quite some time to prepare this castley thing for conferences such as this. We started late in 1969 and we've been expecting you at any time since then. Of course, it's been more than thirty years, so it's become a bit of a project and got grander and more detailed. I think the Air rather likes it. It certainly has all the comforts you could wish for,' said Hamish.

'Sure and wait and see the food we have for you, it's as yummy as a yummy thing, sure it is!' Ned added.

Ned and Hamish were very much in the image of Sionan and spoke with almost the same accent, though their voices were pitched at least two octaves higher. Off their horses they stood about eighteen inches tall, proportionally about the size they had all been while aboard *Ice Dancer*.

They arrived at a turreted corner and began to mount a wide staircase. It took some effort for Ned and Hamish to do this, literally climbing up each step. At the top was a round anteroom with three doorways leading off.

'There's a room for each of you. Your names are on the doors. Prudence, I've put you in with Olga. There are bathrooms attached to each room. I'm sure you'll all need to get a hot bath and some rest. I'll sound a gong for dinner in a few hours.'

'Will the Air be wanting to see us before dinner?' asked Sionan.

'He'll talk with you at dinner,' said Ned.

Ned and Hamish wandered off down the stairs bickering affectionately in a way that only true old friends can, saying honestly whatever irritated them, without ever invoking any breach of the solid trust that existed between them.

'See, Hamish – you'll never understand humour, you either have it or you don't,' Ned muttered, as they walked away.

Olga was thinking how much she could use some space. It had been a long journey and quite the most powerful experience in her life. She was also thinking that never in her whole life had she felt quite so smelly and scruffy. What she needed most was a long soak in a hot bath, and she was grateful for the Air's insight. They went off into their rooms with barely another word. Olga walked through another door into the bathroom where a hot steaming bath awaited her. She abandoned the clothes she had worn for the whole voyage and got into the bubbly hot water. She almost fell asleep in the bath and lingered till the water started to cool. Leaving the bath, she wrapped herself in the soft white dressing gown which was nearby and walked back into the bedroom. She noticed that Prudence had found herself a corner and was fast asleep, her paws twitching to whatever dream she was enjoying. The bed was made of the same warm, soft cloud they arrived on. She sank into its softness and slept.

CHAPTER NINETEEN

There was a loud gong, a very loud gong. Prudence jumped to her feet and leapt onto Olga's cloud. At almost exactly that moment, Olga awoke and sat upright. She had slept so deeply that for a few seconds she wondered where she was, then it all came flooding back to her – the whole journey, Yiptop, Sionan, Vaa and Hmk, the Air, the Moon, Hamish and Ned, and Prudence, who was presently almost on top of her, wagging her tail in excitement and happiness. Also flooding back to her was the join, as she called it: she had just remembered who she was now, and she could remember who she used to think she was before all these revelations and discoveries. Between them was the join. It was as if two parts had been put together as one thing, but you could still see the join. Olga was not at all uncomfortable being Angel of the Moon, and previously being just Olga had been fine too. Being both would be easier if it were not for the join being so evident. The join sort of amplified the separation between the two. Olga was at the same time thinking that maybe joins were normal, and that maybe this join was not exclusive to her own very special situation. Previous to all that had happened, didn't she and indeed everyone live with a join? Maybe even a more complicated join, and one that became more, not less, apparent as time went by, and almost becoming a trap they could fall into. People were born with the simplicity of who they were, then as they got a bit older they started to have an image of who they and the people around them thought that they should be. As they went on through life the gap could widen and they would risk falling into the gap never really knowing who they were.

With all the changes that were occurring in Olga's mind, her memory was becoming very much clearer – she remembered the lightness of simply being, the effortlessness of existence in that simplicity. She remembered this from long ago, from when she was so young that not even language had yet sullied the simplicity of thought. Olga planned to work on the join, she planned to relax into just being, and rise above any kind of pressure, internal or external – she was Olga, Angel of the Moon. All of this could be one, and acceptance was the key to this, acceptance and being, in all its great simplicity.

Yiptop heard the gong at the same time. It didn't wake him because he never slept, but it brought him quite abruptly from his peaceful thoughts into a rather sudden, and for him, surprisingly complete and simple feeling that he was at home, returned to his home planet, back to his roots, to the place his people were taken from, all that time ago. Like the prodigal son, he had returned to the aid of his forefathers. Yiptop no longer felt like an outsider; Sionan and Olga were his people as he was their people.

Sionan was already awake when he heard the gong. No such introspective philosophy was abuzz in his mind. It was a long time ago that Sionan had become well accustomed to who he was and his part in the scheme of things. In many ways, Sionan's part in all of this, although perhaps not easier, was less unbalancing for him than it was for the others. Sionan had been waiting for this for a long time.

'Would you all join me in the round room?' came the voice of Hamish. 'The Air will be ready to see you in the dining hall.'

They all got ready and went into the round room where they said their good mornings.

'Hamish, I can't find teddy and the Post anywhere, and we'll need them to be with us,' said Olga.

'Don't you be worrying now. We've been working very hard while you were sleeping. Teddy and the Post are already in the dining hall. The Air was insistent that there be residuals present to record all that happens,' said Hamish.

'Thank you, Hamish,' said Olga.

'Now I am here to tell you that not everything has gone to plan as the Air would have wanted,' said Hamish.

'It's a terrible worry, to be sure it is!' said Ned woefully.

'Now will you shut up and stop with your worrying people like that, Ned! Sure what am I going to do with you!' Hamish exclaimed crossly.

'It's a worry, sure it is!' Ned retorted.

'Ned, it's our job to make these people comfortable, not worry them! Now will you keep your thoughts to yourself?' said Hamish.

'As the cat seems to be out of the bag, why don't you just tell us what's going on? Maybe then we won't need to worry,' said Sionan.

'Well you see, it's like this. The Air had a plan. It was all worked out in every detail, because the Air is quite meticulous. But now a greater power has intervened and we don't know what's going on,' said Hamish.

'Sure it's a terrible worry!' said Ned.

'I'll not tell you again! Will you stop all that?' said Hamish, reaching out to clip Ned around the ear, and missing as Ned ducked.

'There is only one greater power,' said Sionan.

'The Moon,' said Olga.

'No, not the moon,' said Sionan. 'The moon is of equal power. Only the Gods themselves are of greater power.'

'The gods!' said Olga.

'He's right,' said Hamish.

'Sure and it's a terrible...' Ned started, ducking to avoid another clip from Hamish.

'If the Gods are intervening directly, this is serious to be sure, and I'll admit to some sympathy with Ned and his worries,' said Sionan.

'Now did you not hear the man?' said Ned, at last feeling vindicated.

'Why should it be so worrying?' Olga asked.

'My Angel, when the power of creation itself directly intervenes, it has to be worrying,' said Sionan.

'Yes, I'm worried too,' said Yiptop.

'Do you see now the worry you've caused with all your nonsense, Ned?' said Hamish, a little more annoyed.

'Well, I'm not worried,' said Olga.

'Not worried?' Sionan and Yiptop said together.

'No. I *was* worried, but I'm not now,' Olga confirmed.

'Would you like to bring us up to speed so that we can share your solace?' asked Sionan.

'It's obvious,' said Olga. 'We didn't know what was going to happen, and now we know the world will be saved.'

'How?' asked Yiptop.

'Simplicity,' said Olga.

'Then how is it that only you seem to know this? I can't help feeling everyone has a dose of the riddles since we got here,' said Sionan.

'I should have realised when Hamish and Ned said that they were sent by the gods,' said Olga. Sionan and Yiptop looked at her expectantly.

'The gods created this world. For millions upon millions of years the only direct action they seem to have taken is by the removal of people to colonise other worlds, as we know from Yiptop and the Inuit. Now we learn that this world has threatened universal continuance. We have also learned that there is a predetermined procedure, laid down by the gods, to deal with these circumstances. That procedure is the immediate removal of moon radiation, followed by a pause, during which the moon has the opportunity to bring order to the planet, which is why we are all here.

If that order cannot be reinstated, then the Air leaves the planet and it perishes. The end, for this world, but universal continuance is safe again. So, why would the Gods bother to intervene directly unless they have a reason to save this world? It could be left to perish, without any intervention from them.'

'Sure, she's right, you know!' said Sionan.

'Yes, she is right. They would have no need to be here, if it were not to save the earth. The air is perfectly capable, and duty bound to end it without reference to the gods. If they are here, it's in an attempt to save it,' said Yiptop.

'Yes. And we don't use concepts like *attempt* where the Gods are concerned. If they are minded to save this earth, then they will,' said Sionan.

'Yes, but why?' Yiptop asked.

'Now don't be starting with why, or we'll never finish,' said Sionan. 'If the Gods mean us to know why, then soon enough they will tell us.'

'We should be getting to the dining hall,' said Hamish. 'The Air and maybe even the Gods await our presence.'

They descended the stairs and walked in to the dining hall. When they got in Olga saw teddy and the post in the corner.

'Hi, teddy,' said Olga.

'Hi Olga. This is getting very serious, isn't it? Are you okay?'

'I know, but I'm fine, thanks.,' Olga replied.

'Hi everyone,' said the post. 'I am honoured to be here with you all. Thank you for bringing me.'

'Thank you, post,' said Olga. 'It was you who realised, wisely, who I was, and what we must all do.'

They took their places and realised that there were two more places as yet unoccupied.

'Who are the two places for?' asked Yiptop.

'There are two more guests arriving any minute now,' said Hamish. 'Please wait while I attend to them.'

Hamish and Ned scuttled away leaving all of them in the dining hall. Gentle music started to fill the room. The gentleness of the music transformed the mood of the room from one of great mental activity to a quiet contemplative atmosphere. Olga had always known that music could do that, but never before had she so fully experienced the effect. They bathed in the mind-soothing beauty of the sound and patiently awaited the arrival of two more guests.

CHAPTER TWENTY

Hamish and Ned walked back into the dining hall.

'Dear people, spirits and residuals,' Hamish said in his best ceremonial voice. 'Please welcome the protectors of the domain of the Air, Vaa and Hmk.'

There was the hugging and shaking of hands like old friends, but not just like old friends, but rather like people who had shared, and were sharing, a deep and life changing experience.

'How did you get here, Hmk?' Olga asked.

'Pink cloud of course, darling. It is simply the only way to travel,' Hmk replied with a smile.

A bell rang, not a loud bell, but a bell which demanded attention, a bell which even in the simplicity of its peal spoke volumes. The bell said, 'Observe solemn silence, for what is about to happen is truly of creation itself.'

Olga was thinking how cool was it that a simple bell could say so much. The room fell silent. A pin dropping would have brought pain to the ears of the deaf, such was the quality of silence.

'Welcome, all of you. You will know by now that things have changed and I will no longer be conducting the first part of these proceedings. Shortly the Gods of Creation themselves will be among us. I will only speak again at their direct request,' said the unmistakeable voice of the air.

The hall fell silent again. From the distance came a sound of movement, of feet padding – not clumping; heavy yet light. It approached, getting louder but still gentle. Barely fitting through the ample doorway, it entered the hall, moving with the power of a mighty warrior, yet with the grace of a ballerina. Gliding with feline symmetry, a vision of physical perfection and beauty, each step taking it some great distance across the hall, but with the same surefootedness that would lead you to imagine that the very same movement could with incredible ease be repeated on a tightrope. A magnificent Siberian white tiger sat facing them, its great head reaching at least six feet. The hypnotic, piercing amber eyes – not ice cold, but warm and captivating – held them like rabbits frozen in the beam of a flashlight, staring at each one of them, taking them in, soaking them up. No-one moved, not even Prudence – not even a twitch. They were spellbound by the sheer power and beauty, riveted by the opulent perfection of a creature whose greatness would tempt you to accuse nature itself of self indulgence for its creation.

'Fear not your creator any more than you would fear your own mother. I am the mother of everything you experience, the mother of your very existence.' The tiger did not speak – the voice came from inside their own minds, but the tiger was connected with it. It was as if the tiger was speaking to them with some kind of telepathy.

'There are matters to discuss, yet so great is the distance between our perspectives, that it will take all the concentration within you to understand.'

Olga held up her hand.

'Olga, you wish to speak. Please do.'

'Are you the god of all creation?' Olga asked.

'It would make more sense for you to see me as part of the Gods of all creation, although in my plane of existence, singular and plural have no relevance, as do time and place. For you, the simple answer would be yes, Olga. I am that,' said the voice.

'But you look like a tiger,' said Olga.

'It is my understanding that you are more comfortable with an image. The tiger is not I, nor I the tiger. For visual focus, I chose what I find to be the earthly creation of greatest visual symmetry, a symbol of power and beauty, grace and elegance. Was it not your mind that was tempted to accuse me of self-indulgence for its creation?' said the voice of the gods.

'So you know what is in our minds before we speak?' said Olga.

'Of course. I know at all times what is in all your minds. I do you the courtesy of allowing you to express yourselves in your own way, as it will serve to retain your balance in this difficult situation.'

'Thank you,' said Olga. 'The accusation was not meant to offend.'

'It did not,' said the voice of the gods.

'What does this mean, that you trouble yourself to come here?' Sionan asked.

'It means this. In this particular dimension of creation there are over four hundred billion inhabited planets. This one has become a threat to the continuance of this universe. If this were any other planet, it would have ceased to hold life by now. A pre-determined plan exists for this eventuality. But this is not any other planet. This is the first planet of creation, the very beginning of life in this dimension. All others are derived from life which has evolved on this planet, by what you would call natural evolution. This is the only planet which has been allowed to evolve naturally from the most basic elements. All others were started from human life, with preset parameters for their progress. It would not be possible for the others to have come into existence without the natural development that has occurred on this one. You see, within your dimension, this earth is the beginning of life itself. It has grown to become what it is, with no interference, and it has become the most advanced of all planets.'

'The most advanced!' said Yiptop.

'Yes. I see your misconception; it will pass in time. It will not be I who will relieve you of it, but your growth of understanding what is real. I could speak for a thousand years of the purpose of your lives, the purpose of this universe. Questions would very quickly be raised about your souls, the journey of this life, and the many subsequent lives through which you may pass in your soul's journey towards the dimension of the gods. These questions would then continue to examine the finite nature of this whole universe and all its dimensions. Alas, none of this will even fall within your conceptual parameters, and rightly so: it is already sufficient that you should begin to understand some of your own lives before they end. It is therefore sufficient that you accept that your life has a part in everything, and that you have the journey of this life to complete, and that in the next you will know more.'

'How can this planet continue if it compromises universal continuance?' asked Hmk.

'Good question, and let us not stray further from this subject. It will have to continue, as it is part of a greater plan. It is intrinsic to the purpose of this dimension. It has however reached the point at which it can no longer continue without some government. For the purpose of this government I have chosen four people and one messenger – Sionan, Spirit of Leprechaun; Olga, Angel of the Moon; Yiptop, Hakan of Zog, and Hmk, Spirit of Creation. Prudence, Spirit of Moondog – you will now be Messenger of the Gods. You will all be endowed with the powers you need to fulfil the tasks before you,' said the voice of the gods.

'What will be these powers? Sionan asked.

'These powers will be discovered within yourselves, as they are needed – as Olga has already experienced.

It is Hmk who will know from the Air when intervention is required, and you will all work together to carry out your tasks. Prudence will report each intervention to me via the Moon. We need not discuss much further as I know what is in your minds. I know that you have all understood that this world was created to function autonomously, I know that you have understood that it is not your function to create some utopian society and end human suffering. I know that you have understood that such an effort – although it may seem, when naivety shines, to be desirable – would be utterly counterproductive to the very function of your lives. There will be times when your intervention is required and it will be known by Hmk. I have spoken enough. I see in your minds that it would not be good to continue. You have before you the Gods of Creation: question upon question are raised in your minds. You have your lives to live here.

You must trust that if I could speak further, then I would. The Air can continue and put in place what is required. Before you ask, I will answer this one question: yes, at the end of your journey we will be together again, all of us. Know this, for beyond that knowledge you can have no understanding. I know that you will all do what is required of you. You have all proven on your journey to this place that you would give your lives for the purpose of continuance. There is no more that you could give. Yours is to do all you can in this world – complicated, I admit, by your knowledge of universal continuance.'

The voice paused.

'Residuals, you will see to it that all of this is conveyed to the trees. I must admit that even we gods find them at best difficult to deal with. I will leave you with the love of a mother to her child and in the capable instruction of the Air.'

The tiger left the dining hall, the castle, and the world.

They all relaxed visibly, released from their state of heightened concentration.

'Hamish and Ned, bring food and drink for all, so that they may eat and recover from their audience with the gods. After, we will discuss what is to be done,' said the voice of the Air.

A great feast was presented. They all ate and drank. Sionan was treated to his promised pint of Guinness. Yiptop drank water and enjoyed the happiness the others gained from eating. During the great feast, Hamish and Ned entertained them, Hamish with a beautiful rendition on the harp of some of the most captivating melodies from O'Carolan, known by Leprechauns to be music of the gods. Ned attempted conjuring tricks and jokes – which were really only funny because they were so incongruous in that situation.

At the end of the feast the Air spoke.

'Your task is simplicity itself. Olga, I have been given

the power to return you to your home in Cardiff. Your

parents will of course believe that you returned with

them from their holiday. The gods have over-ridden

Hakan's memory device. You will continue your life

and education as before.'

The Air turned to Sionan and Hmk.

'Sionan, I am empowered to send you and *Ice Dancer*

to Cardiff Bay, where suitable arrangements are in

place for you to continue your life near Olga. Hmk,

you too I am sending to Cardiff, where arrangements

have been made for you to take up an academic

position at the university. A home has been arranged

for you in the same street as Olga. You will be

accepted by Olga's family as a friend and will be

responsible for her education and development.

'Prudence, you will live in the home of Olga, where

you will be remembered by all as the family dog of

long-standing. As appointed Messenger of the Gods, you will be instrumental in conveying information to the Moon and myself.'

'Post, I will return you to the park in Cardiff, where you will take up your usual place and duties. Teddy, you have exchanged all information with the post and are now a fully-informed residual. You will remain with Olga where you will be an invaluable source of information. Vaa, you will return to your people, where you will continue to protect my domain.

'I have made available a permanent consciousness which via Prudence, will be available to you all at all times. You will come to know your great powers as and when you need them. Be assured that they will be formidable. Nothing will ever have the power to get in the way of your work. But heed this warning – seek not an instrument of evil which works against you, for no such singular entity exists. The evil you will fight lies in the potential of each human being. That which any man need ever fear lies within his own weakness; he need only be truly aware of that weakness in order to know the potential evil of others.

'In a few minutes you will all awaken in your places. You will be confused at first, but it will pass quickly.

'One last thing, the Gods have asked me to tell you this, Olga. You have been granted one wish. The Gods know what that wish is, though as yet you do not. You will in time realise what this is. It has, however, already been granted and carried out.'

CHAPTER TWENTY ONE

Emily's operation was unsuccessful. She had returned from the hospital with her parents and there had been much upset and anger. The usually happy and contented home had yet to adjust to the situation. The current plan was for Emily to return to her usual school. This had been decided on the basis of the belief that it would be better for her to retain as much normality as possible. It was also Emily's insistence that she be among her friends – particularly Olga, who she felt she needed now more than ever.

Emily was sitting at her bedroom window, it was a clear night and the moon was full. Unbeknown to Emily it was also, for the first time in many years, a moon fully functioning. Already, after only a short period of deafness, Emily had started to notice a heightening of awareness in her other senses – it was as if somehow a compensation was occurring, and she could see and smell better. Emily was looking at the moon in all the wonder of its fullness. She could see it with an uncanny clarity as if through a telescope. The blue white silvery surface, the rich greyness in the darker places and the almost yellow luminescence, almost warming like a more delicate and subtle daughter of the sun. Emily was bathing in the moonbeams. As she was bathing, she felt a sensation in her ears – not a pain, but a feeling that the whole of her inner ear had a sensation of being. She could feel the shape of it, from the opening down to her eardrum, and then movement, growth: something was happening. This lasted a minute or so, then the sensation left her. She turned away from the window, and as she did so, she knocked the vase of flowers to the floor with her elbow. As they hit the floor, she heard the crash. For a second, but only a second, she thought 'Oh, no! Mum's vase! I've broken it!' That second passed about as slowly as a second can. Then she stood up and ran to the door and down the stairs to the living room where her mum and dad were sitting.

'Mum! Dad! I can hear, really! Something has happened! I can hear. I knocked the vase off the window sill and I heard it fall. I heard it clearly. I can hear, I really can hear! Say something, speak to me!'

'Darling! Can you hear me, can you really hear me?' said her dad.

'Yes, clearly – just like I used to, no different,' said Emily.

'This is impossible! How?' said Emily's dad.

'No,' said Emily's mum, tears in her eyes, 'it's not impossible. It's happened.'

Terry Wogan was playing 'Once in a very Blue Moon' sung by Nancy Griffiths. Even in her confused state, Olga didn't miss the significance and refused to accept coincidence.

'Teddy, did all that happen?'

'All what?' teddy replied.

'You know all what, teddy!' said Olga.

'Only joking,' said teddy. 'Look who's coming.'

Prudence had got up from the corner of the room and was walking over to Olga and teddy wagging her tail.

'Good morning,' came into Olga's mind, in much the same way as the words of the Gods had.

'Prudence, you can speak to me! Amazing! What's all that about?' Olga exclaimed.

'I suppose the Gods reasoned that there was no point in a messenger who can't pass on a message,' came Prudence's telepathic reply.

'Olga! Time for school, darling. The bathroom's free,' Olga's dad shouted.

'Breakfast's ready,' Olga's mum called from downstairs.

Olga opened her bedroom door and Prudence trundled downstairs.

''Morning, Pru. Want to go outside, do you?' said Olga's mum.

Prudence went out into the garden, just like any dog would on a Monday morning.

Olga got washed and dressed and went downstairs for her breakfast just like any ten-year-old girl would on a Monday morning. In fact, not anything like Angel of the Moon.

'A lot's been happening while we were away,' said Olga's dad.

'Like what?' said Olga.

'I was chatting to Emily's dad on the phone last night, after you'd gone to bed. They were involved an awful accident by the park. Apparently that idiot cousin of yours was involved,'
said Olga's dad.

'Is Emily okay?' Olga asked.

'Yes. Well she is now, anyway. So are her mum and dad. Your cousin Arnie is okay too, amazingly, though two of his friends died.'

'It's good that Arnie's okay,' said Olga.

'It is,' said Olga's dad. 'But it won't be long before he has another go at killing himself, or someone else, the way he carries on.'

'What do you mean by *she is now* – did she get hurt?'

'She completely lost her hearing. Everyone was very worried about her. She was in hospital for a while and had an operation without success. Then suddenly last night, her hearing came back. Emily swears it has something to do with the moon. Her dad's not so sure about that, but it does seem quite miraculous.'

'It's exactly what I would have wished for her,' said Olga with a satisfied smile.

'You'd better get off to school, then. You'll see her – she apparently insisted on going today. She's told everyone how much she missed you. Is Pru going with you as usual?' said Olga's mum.

'Yes… Er, that's what she usually does, isn't it?'

'You know she loves nothing more than to hang around outside school for you to come out, funny old thing that she is,' said Olga's mum.

'Look,' said Olga's dad looking through the front window. 'A removal van. Must be someone new moving into number forty three.'

Olga went to the window in time to see Hmk talking with the people in the removal van. She looked different without her arctic clothing.

'Nice to have new people. We should see if there's anything she needs,' said Olga's mum.

'Oh, can I do that after school? Please, mum!' Olga asked.

'Okay, but I'll come with you, to see what they're like,' said Olga's mum.

'Looks like a young lady living alone,' said Olga's dad.

'I'm off to school, then. come on Prudence,' said Olga, calling Prudence in from the garden.

They both went off down the street. Olga had hoped to bump into Hmk on the way, but she was inside the house. She also thought about going past the park to see if the Post was okay, but decided to do that on the way home instead.

Olga settled into the classroom. She hadn't seen Emily in the playground, and was wondering where she had got to. She arrived a few minutes late and ran over to Olga.

'Olga! I've got so much to tell you!' she said, hugging Olga.

'I know! My mum and dad told me this morning. Are you really okay?' Olga asked.

'I am now, but it was really horrible being deaf. It was the moon, Olga – my mum says that's silly, but I know it was the moon. It me back my hearing last night,' Emily insisted.

'Emily, strange things happen, and if you think it was the moon, who can say different? The main thing is that you're okay,' said Olga.

'You know your mad cousin Arnie was involved, and two of his friends were killed,' said Emily.

'Yes, I know,' said Olga. *I'll be having a word with him very soon*, she thought.

The school day passed uneventfully. Olga was thinking that perhaps from now on, a lot of things would seem uneventful, after everything she had been through over the holidays. When it was time to go home, she met Prudence outside the school gates, where she was patiently waiting.

'We must go to the Post on the way back,' Prudence pathed to her. 'Yiptop, Hmk and Sionan will meet us there.'

'Cool. I was hoping we'd see them soon,' said Olga.

They walked towards the park. It was a nice day, not sunny, but not windy or raining. As they arrived at the corner of the park, Olga could see the unmistakeable and familiar silhouettes of Sionan, Hmk and Yiptop standing by the Post, who was now reinstated in his original position. She ran up to them and Sionan picked her up with a big, enveloping hug.

'Sure, it's good to see you, my Angel,' he said, smiling warmly, his deep reverberating voice almost tickling her ears.

They all hugged and said hello. Yiptop looked more human than ever in his now-familiar skateboarder's clothes.

'I'm all moved in now, and already we have work to do, very soon,' said Hmk.

'What work is that?'

'There is a nasty situation in Korea and it's getting out of hand. We will get together this week, and see what needs to be done,' said Hmk.